I0666768

Marzia Palombi

Mizzy's Diary

How to Have Some Fun, Make Lots of Money and Find True Love in Just Thirty Days!

Youcanprint *Self-Publishing*

Title | MIzzy's Diary

Author | Marzia Palombi

ISBN | 978-88-93217-05-7

© All rights reserved to the Author

No part of this book may

be reproduced without the

Prior consent of the author.

Youcanprint Self-Publishing

Via Roma, 73 – 73039 Tricase (LE) – Italy

www.youcanprint.it

info@youcanprint.it

Facebook: facebook.com/youcanprint.it

Twitter: twitter.com/youcanprintit

MEETING Mizzy

I met Mizzy when she had already crossed the "Plupart" of the troubles of her life. At that time, she was a woman in her thirties who was happily engaged and successfully running her own business. We met at a party. She was tall and thin, a beautiful woman, with dark wavy hair, provocatively dressed in a short skirt and a nice black décolleté. Everyone had turned their head to look at her when she entered the room with her man on her side.

She looked really sensual. Even if she had been dressed in a turtleneck and a pair comfortable jeans, many men in there would have certainly noticed her. The two parted soon after they came in: he headed towards his host friends, she was alone, in the middle of male attention and female envy. I got curious and started to chit-chat with her. After this first meeting, many others followed. After we became close friends, she filled me in on some facts of her life.

Later on she had me read about it! She had a collection of diaries that were gathrerd fragments of her past, stories of a special nature I guess. "Her adventures" were so striking to me right from the first pages leaving me in dibelief!

It seemed impossible to me that she could have lived through so many experiences. Maybe I showed her such a sincere enthusiastic interest in her past that Mizzy decided to give me

an unexpected gift: "Make a book out of my diary!".

She did so hoping I could become a

writer. For this and for her friendship I'll thank her all life. Mizzy was satisfied with her past life. Not He had no regrets! As if her past had contributed to create her present: a present that still gave her joy and satisfaction.

This first diary contained a story truly full of surprises! The first time I read it I thought that Mizzy had made it all up. I changed my mind when she answered my tsunami of questions with lots of special details impossible to make up even for a skilled writer.

This first diary dated back to ten years before, when she

she was only twenty years old. In that period she attended the faculty of literature of the University La Sapienza of Rome. She lived with her parents in an apartment nearby. Mizzy was from "a good family ", and everyone of the had a degree! Her parents, despite having a higher education, weren't good managers of their money: during their life they had accumulated several millions of lires of debts and to pay them they started a mortgage on the value of their apartment. By then they were no longer able to pay the installments. Mizzy, became aware of the problem and decided to do something about it . Joe, a close friend of her's proposed her a "small job" in a night club by the sea of some friends of his. It was late July and Mizzy decided to check it out and start working ...

*

... Since it actually is my first book, I looked for a shoulder that would somehow support me ... MY HUSBAND! THE SECOND ONE! But, given his unforgivable stick-in-the-mud comments that I decided to share with my loyal readers (if they aren't yet, I hope they will soon become such) ... I discovered, to my great surprise that, alas, I could be in search of the third one sooner than I thought! Throughout the story, I wanted to include his pearls of wisdom to enrich my endeavor! Judge for yourself ... your thoughts, comments, gossip and everything else will be extremely welcome, useful and constructive ... if you will do me the honor of sharing them on my blog: **mizzylove.com**. *Thanks and happy reading!*

THE TRIP

July 28

Today a lot of sensational events took place! *Considering that*

Mizzy thought everything was "great" or "lousy" depending on her mood, we ought to reconsider the magnitude of the adjective "sensational" ... Of course, it's a known fact that all Sagittarians are lunatics! Luckily, after much insistence, I went to see Joe. What can I say about him... he is a man about thirty-five years old, looks a little bit like the singer Zucchero, I've known him for years ... he came into my life through my mother's work, a teacher; He was a friend of one of his student's sister. *Quite a complicated situation I would say! But let's move on.* I can add that he's the first guy I kissed, but for educational purposes only! The fact is that he practically nipped in the bud my showbiz dreams of a career as an actress. Not because he didn't think much of my acting skills, but because he thought that to be an actress you had to give yourself away to practically everyone. He had been inviting me for months to Bellaria to meet a friend of his when I finally found the courage to jump on a train and get there. *Nowadays it takes a lot of courage to get on a train*! At the station there was my friend Joe waiting for me! *A friend to me? Joe might have actually believed he was, but if he thought there was something that wasn't supposed to be done, he immediately told Mizzy not to do it ... that way he was sure that she would! What a lunatic!* Together we went straight to meet his friend Remo, at the beach resort where he worked. Joe had been hassling me for months with the story of this encounter. I had never taken neither Joe nor his stories seriously! I joined him more to work rather than to meet his friend. But, I had to think again.

THE ENCOUNTER

Wow! I didn't expect to meet such a cool guy: Remo is one meter and eighty five centimers tall, over five centimeters taller than me, and very tanned. *Keen observation, it is extremely rare to find a tanned man who works in a beach resort!* Black hair, blue eyes, muscular, a real hunk. He liked me immediately and so did I. He was kind, he treated me to ice cream, we chatted for a half hour, but there was Joe too. At one point, Joe left us alone so Remo told me: "Listen, do you think that when I come back to Rome in September, I can ask you out ? Would you like it?" I don't remember what I answered him, but it must have been something like this: "Sure! Sure! All right! etc." This proposal excited me a bit. *Perhaps Remo did not understand that you had gone to Bellaria not for him but for the job you had to do and he was only 1% of the reasons for your trip. Be patient he is a bit dumb! But maybe you hadn't realized it yourself! You can't have everything in life ... that's what frustrated people say ... and they are, in fact, the vast majority of the ones you come across!*

THE JOB

After we had met, I went, accompanied by Joe and Remo, to see what this famous job was about. *Mizzy had never worked seriously: as most girls of her age, she had worked the usual jobs: babysitter, cleaning woman, maid and ironing clothes, the job she was maybe best at. A real passion!* They took me right up to the open door of this Night Club. *Surprise!* There they handed me to a "shady character" with whom I would go throgh the job interview. *Obviously for this kind of work there is no need to go through a real job interview: the essential thing in nightclubs is to be a female, although sometimes transvestites are rated higher than young ladies.* He certainly wasn't a handsome man: obese, ugly, to say the least and sweaty to top it all! I was a little embarrassed! After I was introduced, he noticed my stunned expression so he took me into a private room! We were alone. That's where I had my personal job interview. It lasted a minute! The "shady character" asked me: "If a customer puts his hands here what will you do?" and while he asked me, he put his hand in my most forbidden place. My heart started racing out of control! I gathered all my courage and I mirrored his gesture even more explicitly. I surprised him! Perhaps he probably thought he was dealing with the girl next door! He offered me an easy and very well paid job: a million and a half liras every two weeks just to talk with men that would be at the club. I would try to keep them talking to me as long as possible. They pay a "fixed amount" every twenty minutes to offer drinks to us girls who are there waiting for them. We girls get a percentage of every dirk the customer buys us, and that adds up to the bi-weekly pay. It is a job that I can handle comfortably and I really need a lot of cash, so I think I will do it! My parents are in debt. I want to help them pay for my university degree. Although our relationship is not the best now, I owe them at least that for all they have done for me! I will try to help them economically. I feel almost compelled to accept this job! Today I would do anything for money except hurting others, because I know how it feels to have empty pockets, and that's a feeling I don't want to experience ever again! After these clarifications the "shady character" "let me leave" and I went back to the beach resort where Joe and Remo were waiting for me. The night club and the beach resort are very close to one another, a three minute walk I would say. I'm in seventh heaven! Let's face the truth … perhaps this meeting upset you a little! With only one trip, I killed two birds with one stone: I got a job and I met a charming guy. After that, I spent some time chatting with Joe and Remo on the beach. I'm starting my job in August, and I just can't stop thinking about it! And this is just the beginning of the trauma that nightlife can have on a, naive or perhaps more properly, helpless young girl!

COMING BACK HOME

They both saw me off at the train station, and Joe came back to Rome with me. Remo was very sweet to me; who knows ... maybe he really thought we'd meet again in September. During the whole trip I kept on talking about him to Joe and I really think I drove him crazy! The fact is that when I'm fixed on a topic I can't manage to talk about anything else. I think I have a huge crush on him; let's hope for the best. I didn't have much luck with men in the past. Joe gave me some good advice: "Let him be the one who makes the first move, don't act as you usually do running after him! I could very well give you his phone number, but you'd better be sure he's really interested in you, right?". I had to admit he was right. My parents don't know anything about this job and hopefully they never will. Mizzy's parents were a little reckless with money so they had lost five family homes to satisfy each one of their daughter's little whim and they were also paying a mortgage on the one in which they were living in. He had a temporary job as a proofreader in a small newspaper, and she was high school teacher, the actual breadwinner. Finally we arrived in Rome, I got off at Tiburtina station and I I went straight home by bus. I arrived late and I started to write my diary, I stayed up so late ... it was crazy!

FIRST LIES

July 29, Sunday

Today I woke up comfortably at 10:30. *As if Mizzy woke up much earlier on normal days. She was used to waking up at about 9:30.* I started to pack. As soon as I go back to Bellaria I'll start working. I told my folks I had found a job in a hotel on the coast and that I'd call every night to tell them all those reassuring things a good daughter ought to tell her parents to brighten up their nights. *Why aren't you just saying that you don't wan't them to have nightmares over you!* Luckily, it all went well and they believed every word I said, I really am an excellent actress. Anyway, they are too busy to thinking about their own stews to actually check on me! Before leaving I'll have to tidy up my room a bit: just semblance of order, nothing more. Of course I packed my whole stock of pills: Algae of all types, stems of pineapple, diet pills, etc ... *Mizzy was terrorized of assimilating food, so before she had any food at all, she stuffed herself with all sorts of pills. Well! It would have been simpler to be careful about what she ate. Who knows, maybe this solution was too simple for her.* Too bad! I only have a couple of swim suits; if I get a chance, I'll get a few more when I get there. With the kind of work I'm going to do I will surely need sexy clothes, and most of all proper shoes. I always dress like a tomboy! This is not to say that I like women. *As it was noted by the disproportionate reaction to the "first comer".* No! They just do not interest me! They merely talk about clothes and "stupid" things; men are definetely more interesting! Oh, I forgot the most important thing that happened at lunch: Remo phoned; He asked Joe to give him my number and then called me up, isn't it incredible? He asked me how my return trip was. We chatted about this and that, then he confessed that he was happy to have met me! Fantastic! I'm really happy too! He sounds like a good guy: he's kind, caring; let's hope it's not just appearance to impress. I heard from Joe and I told him about the phone call. He seemed jealous … he's really stupid! He was the one to insist! For months, he wanted me to go Bellaria to meet his friend. Who knows … maybe he didn't like the fact that Remo called me the very first day after we met. Too bad for Joe! So now he'll know better to have two people meet when he actually doesn't want them to get to know each other!

PREPARATIONS

July 30, Monday

Today I went to do some shopping; I really love it! I bought all the pills I needed and I was missing at the Herbalist's Pharmacy, some mosquito spray and the stick you need after they bite. I hate mosquitoes! I also got a nice black evening dress. I tried to match it with a pair of low heel, seemingly (and luckily) comfortable "almost" evening shoes! I'm not used to high heels, they make my feet hurt immediately, in fact I never wear them.

It's strange because if I dress like a real woman (short skirt, heeled shoes, etc …) men run after me (is it maybe because I have long legs ?!) *Or is it because men all react the same way to women ?!* But despite of that, I feel most comfortable when I wear casual clothes. Shopping gets me really tired! It's already late in the afternoon and Remo hasn't called me today. Has something bad happened? Am I perhaps a bit paranoid? *What are you thinking … it's normal for a man you just met to call you every two hours, three at the most!* Tonight there is a good movie on television and I'll try to not think about it. I won't call him, first of all because I don't have his telephone number and second because I won't ask Joe, otherwise who knows what he might do! The date of my departure is approaching and I am a bit nervous, August the first also coincides with the start of my new job. I'm through writing for today, I'm really tired!

July 31, Tuesday

I bet he'll call today! 4 p.m: he phoned! Miracle! I told him that I accepted the job. He thinks that we're only girls serving at the tables and at most, we have a friendly chat with the customers. I wish it were so, but I really don't think so. Is it possible that there are men that feel so lonely that they pay just to talk with women? Whatever you think Remo, I don't see him looking too worried about it and this is basically what matters. I certainly won't be the one to tell him the detais of what happens to me every day. *You've never been a source of absolute truth, and it won't be difficult for you to lie, right?* It actualy will be difficult, I really am quite a talker, but if I talk all night, it is likely that during the daytime I'll do something else ... Moreover, Remo told me that as long as he works at the Beach resort, he can set me up in his apartment where he is living now. It's spacious enough and he shares it with his employer's two daughters. The apartment is close to the resort and to my night club and above all, we will definitely use it at different hours. We might almost never meet. Tomorrow is the big day, the beginning! I look forward to seeing Remo. Today nothing special happened, I have been home all day. In the evening I went to see a my friend of mine, we had dinner together and we watched a video together.

DEPARTURE

August 1, Wednesday

Last night I could not fall asleep! This morning I took the train at nine. At Bellaria Station both Remo and the "shady character" came to pick me up. The latter told me that I had to get ready and be at the night club by 10 p.m. , all dressed up for the big event. I called my parents, they were happy, I was brief. I went to lunch with Remo. I must say that I didn't have much of an appetite. The poor guy had taken a day off to stay with me me to get used to the place and to help me set my two suitcases (enormous and overflowing with junk) in the apartment. It's a beautiful, perfectly furnished house; my own house is not among the houses that can afford such luxury. The room that I'm sharing with Remo has two bunk beds. "I will share with you the room," I said, "if I can sleep in the top bed". Be my guest and sleep wherever you please" he said. He is condescending on anything, this is one of my favorite qualities in a man! I was glad to spend so much time with him! In the afternoon we had a trip to town: Bellaria is really pretty! In the evening I got ready and I had dinner with him at the beach resort. It's open from morning until late evening

when the patrons have their dinner, see outdoor movies, play

video games under a large veranda equipped with almost all sorts of distractions; during daytime hours it protects them from the hot sun keeping them somewhat cool. At 9.45 I went to the club.

FIRST NIGHT AT WORK

At the entrance there was the "shady character", another bartender and then me. The first one is hugely fat and when he walks he looks like he is actually rolling! *She has become wicked!* He was dressed in blacks pants and a worn out blue shirt, custom made clothes just for him, but you could tell they were home made and the result was not that good! He gave me the impression of being a slimy guy! *Was it perhaps because he did nothing but sweat and wipe his forehead with a large handkerchief?* But perhaps the first impression is not always the right one. The second guy's name is Max and differently from the other barman he was dressed with blacks slacks, black shirt and wore a red jacket over them. *Practically a punch in the eye!* Here you could easily tell that his clothes were made out of luxurious and expensive fabrics, custom made by a real tailor. Max really impressed me ... immediately! He's not really handsome, but he's got style and he's definetely out of the ordinary!

We were there all alone ...the three of us. The "shady character"

whose name is Marco, introduced me to Max and we all started

talking while waiting for the girls ... *The cannon fodder* ... and the users of the service ... *The unscrupulous and unrefined butchers!* Finally some time after 10, the other girls arrived wearing really flashy clothes, in their perfect make up and smelling real good, it felt lke being in a field of fragrant flowers. I felt a little uncomfortable in my simple dress!

The night seemed endless, it felt like time was paralized

and I looked at the clock every minute! There are some

rules to follow: when the DJ puts Disco music on

all the girls like me who are not in the company of a

customer, have to dance. So men who are looking for company may choose us better. Then another rule is that we must be seated all together on pre established sofas. When we aren't working we can have only a drink throughout the whole evening! We are supposed to dress sexy and if accidentally we are wearing pants, they fine us! Money that will be deducted from our pay. There is also a fine for delays.

I like dancing, that's not a problem! It's like getting free entrance to the disco every night! Before then, I couldn't afford to go there very often, so in a way, this job is somewhat like being at the luna park! Sitting with the other girls is just fine: I'll have to get to know them better and start socializing with them! The only drawback is the drinks, we hope to get many "tables" (jargon of club that means the twenty minutes of consumption in which a customer offers you a drink and sits down to chat with you) ... *I didn't know that satisfying sexual appetites was called chatting* ... Wow, I'm learning the night time jargon! During this long night I exchanged a few words with some girls. I was the only Italian one, the other girls were mostly from Eastern countries. Fortunately, in the end I managed to get a table with two men: the first guy was a bricklayer, he was chubby and during the entire twenty minutes time he did nothing but to lay his hands all over me! An octopus! I felt totally embarrassed, I didn't know how to get him to chat with me and he really didn't care much other than getting some sexual performance from me! Maybe I wasn't able to react the right way because it was the first time I did this work ... I hope to learn fast, otherwise I'm in real trouble! I wish I could bail myself out when the situation gets bad. The second man I got the table with was a clerk and he asked me straight away if we could go out together, but I told him categorically no! He didn't have any class ... *And what are you surprised to! You're not at the Excelsior Hotel even though maybe you would not have found any better in terms of depravation.* I only managed to get two drinks all night! *Like a cow that does not produce any milk!* If I managed to be liked more, I would chat for a longer time and time would fly faster! Instead, last night was boring and endless, I almost fell asleep, also because I'm not used to staying up so late!

THE BEACH RESORT

August 2, Thursday

At 4:00 in the morning I went back to Remo's apartment, I had the keys, I was too tired to take a shower and I climbed on my small bunk bed. Remo sleeps so soundly that he didn't wake up even though I stunk like an ashtray, perhaps because he

smokes and so he was used to such strong odors. However, I couldn't fall to sleep, I tossed and turned in bed until 6:30, when Remo woke up and started getting ready to go to work. Thus, because there was no way I could catch any sleep, I offered to help him at the bar. He agreed, but only for the company. The resort isn't very big but it's quite nice, a bonbonierre. Thirty beach umbrellas can fit on the beach and there is a terrace with tables all to covered by a wicker roof to offer some shade and also a small kitchen. The bathrooms and showers are clean and all work perfectly and there was also a small office where they did all the back office work, and finally, there were many slot machines. We talked a lot about my job and Remo tried to figure out whether it was a good job ... *Yea, right! The girls are all in their place!* ... Fortunately, I managed to convince him it was and so his doubts vanihed just as they appeard. He lured me to breakfast, but my appetite was gone along with my tiredness! Luckily! ... *Poor thing you didn't even notice that the shock has changed your main features: eating a lot and sleeping like a log?* ... So I spent a quiet morning: some time laying out in the sun and the rest sitting behind the counter. Then, the afternoon in the bunk bed reading. In the evening, Remo convinced me to have something to eat. So, after avidly drinking two tall glasses of water, I swallowed several of my pills and then I shared my food with Perlina, the dog of the resort: two equal portions, two burgers; Perlina is a very nice and sweet female dog.

FIRST ILLUSIONS

Unfortunately, it's time to go to work and this time at ten sharp,,

this time, not a minute before, I went to the club. On entering, you can smell a typical odor: It smells like diving into a big ashtray that no one has ever emptied. But after a while, you get used to it and you don't smell it anymore! ... *The typical addiction to ashtray smell, not to smoking!* Today Max is wearing a yellow jacket. I literarly got him involved him into having an embarassing and tight exchange of compliments with me, I couldn't help it ... I'm really attracted to him! Tonight I have to say that work went somewhat better, time went by much quicker. I had a long table with a gentleman who said that he wanted to introduce me to his sister. His name was Claudio. We had a long talk and then he touched me! I let him, and he was the first man ever who I gave permission to, I don't know

why, maybe because he did it in a nice way: I let him put his hand between my thighs, he was handsome, with style, ... I could tell! I loved it! ... *Being touched by money or by that handsome man?* I wanted him to go further but he had to go! He told me he was a wholesale butcher. He made me a strange proposal ... but quite inviting I should say: he asked me to go and move in with him. He would pay me for that. He asked me how much I wanted and I shot really high ... 5 million lire a month! In the end we agreed on to two million and a half. He also told me that if her sister would like me, he would even get married! He promised that he would return the next day to take me out to dinner, and then he asked many questions about what kind of jewelry I liked and I finally, he said he would bring me a bracelet as a gift ... *And donkeys fly!* ... I was sorry that he had to go, I would have gladly spent the entire night and not only letting him touch me! I was excited! It's very difficult to have this effect on me. I also did other tables for more than forty minutes each. The "shady character" helped me out, introducing me as a new girl, the only Italian one, coming up from time to time with smart lines that attracted customers. Towards closing time, I chatted a little with him and I told him about the invitation to dinner I had received. He was really happy for me.

A NEW LOVE IS BORN

August 2, Friday

I went to bed at four in the morning but I got a surprise: Remo was awake! We kissed for a long time and then we made love. it was wonderful! I have to say that the sexual act lasted a lot and Remo is really good at it. *Want to fill us in with details?!* Although I felt really good and I didn't fall asleep after a

night's work and this magical moment with him, I decided to

go to the beach only later, around lunch time, don't ask me why. *Who's asking you?* After my pills, I shared another two burgers with Perlina. I was very happy. I wanted to give a hand and I really insited to do so! and I worked as a bartender with very good results, I must admit. Standing behind the counter I let Karen and Lisa, the two daughters of the owner of the resort, go and have a swim and do gymnastics on the beach, to relax a bit. They are sisters but don't look alike at all: Karen is blonde, slim and petite instead Lisa is a brunette with a ton of cellulite on her thighs, a bit over abundant and big boned ... *You really know how describe people ... without any mercy!* Characterwise, even though I don't know them really well, they both look a bit snobbish. Let's hope for the best ... yes, hope never dies! Remo was very thoughtful as usual, he was nice all day long ... *Having a beautiful female body makes men really thoughtful!* In the afternoon we went in the bathroom used by the staff of the resort and we made love once more. Remo was sitting

on the toilet and I was on top of him. Something strange happened: the toilet seat broke. Luckily he did'nt get hurt ... *With the weight of two people I'm surprised you both didn't sink into the toilet!* ... I like making love! I really felt I cared for him, I would almost say that I love him! *Maybe a tad exaggerated?* When we're together time flies and I'm so happy! At dinner time, that guy didn't show up of course, neither him nor his precious bracelet: I'm beginning to see the fictional world of lies that was around the club ... *You wish you could see it so easily ... with that head of yours buried in the sand!...* Anyway, since I am very passionate and sentimental too, I got offended, although I think it was better that way; Marco, the "shady character" felt real bad for me and Max did too. So they pampered for a while ...*Yea right... to take you to bed and because sad cows are don't make good milk!* I had already used up all of my evening dresses so I was thinking it would be appropriate to get new ones ... *Or maybe it was better to get a fool like Remo to buy them for you?* ... I enjoyed myself a lot at the club, there was always beautiful music and I was more and more attracted to Max to the point that I started a game with him: when he came to me and I was with a client, without him noticing, I touched him. I enjoyed it very much, it was very exciting! He also appreciated it and I dare say very much indeed! It was a nice pastime, and I just wish it had led somewhere... *Why, wasn't Remo the only man in your life? Wasn't he great in and out of bed? What was missing? Maybe it's the atmosphere of the nightclub that went to your head! ...*

I did a few of tables and I was revved up for Max, and so being

much more cheerful, I attracted many more customers. I also started to get acquainted with the other girls; I thought they considered me unpleasant or nasty, instead I found out they were just shy because they didn't speak Italian that well: they were all foreign. Many are working this job to put aside enough money to open a business in their country. They can do that because the Lira is worth much more than the local currency in Eastern European countries, and in many others. That way they manage to save up save astonishing fortunes. Many of the girls of the club hate their work, in fact they are chosen only for their beauty, their fashionable clothes and their refreshing scents. Instead, they choose me for the tables because I took this absurd job as a game, I have fun and men are more attracted to cheerful girls who are full of life!

August 4, Saturday

At four the night's work is over. I went home. This time I woke Remo up to make love, I was too excited. It was great to the point that after I dozed away with him, tightly embraced in a

single bed, we had a great time! In the morning he went to the beach as usual. I took a shower and after three long days and sleepless nights I managed to fall asleep. I woke up at lunchtime. I went for a walk around Bellaria and I headed for the beach. I helped at the bar to pay back my accomodation somehow, I don't want to feel in debt to anyone, let alone

to those two girls that seem so phoney. Today something real bad happened: Karen and Lisa secretly came to the club last night and who knows what they think the saw. It's so dark in there that in spite of my trained eyes from long hours spent in there I often can't see everything myself. So they told Remo that they didn't want me to sleep with them in his uncle's apartment. Remo didn't react to avoid damaging his work relationships that would last until September. What a coward! I don't know whether I'll ever forgive him for this low blow! However, to make up for such a thing he began to look for an alternative. *What were you expecting? Maybe that he would defend you by saying: "She isn't the way you saw her, she's a saint! "* I'm shocked! Firstly because I expected

Remo to defend me to the hilt, *Yea, right!* Secondly because I tried in every way to be helpful at the bar of the resort and for free. They thought I was a prostitute when I hadn't actually done anything of tht sort. *Really nothing?* They want war? So I'll make them all happy! I'm awfully sad, I thought Remo loved me for real and what happened makes me believe that it's not so. Maybe I misjudged Remo, I thought he was a strong, brave man, but deep down inside he's only a coward! They hurt me a lot! It's not right to hurt someone, especially one who has done good work in taking your place for free ... *Yes, human beings are often very disappointing. They don't really look at the person they have in front, but only at the label that society put on you, so if a man is a firefighter he must be a good person, if a woman is a prostitute*

she's definitely someone to be marginalized ... I immediately called Joe who really felt bad about this (He would have never expected such a thing, neither from the girls nor from Remo) and immediately phoned Marco to find a solution. Marco came to the resort and there we put our heads together, including Remo's to come up with an acceptable solution. The first solution Marco came up with was for me to cohabit with the girls working at the club. I turned him down. The second choice was to go to Marco's home and share his eighteen year old daughter's room with her. This choice seemed to be the least harmful, so I accepted. Maybe I would enjoy myself and hopefully she was nice. Remo helped me pack up and then I went with Marco to his house. The new home is a house that reminded me of my own: not too clean, but only because of the mess!

They tried to tidy up every day, but all those things on the floor were always in the way. This lack of order put me at ease. Marco has a wife, Laura, a woman quite a bit overweight, just like him. She reminded me of my mother, who was also a

little abundant. They have three children: Tiziana the eighteen year old one, Simone, thirteen and Luke who's just one year old. It's a strange family, but they're quite easy going. *What does strange mean to you? What family is ever normal?* They are nice and without preconceptions, they are people who look at what people have done before they place judgement, the reasons that pushed them to do what they have done and only after careful analysis they form their opinion. I quickly familiarized with Tiziana, and she gave me half of her own closet to put my clothes in. But since I didn't have many, my new friend decided to open up her wardrobe to me, her make up and to share everything she owned with me, as if we were sisters! I was so happy! I finally had the large family I had always dreamed of being an only child. Tiziana is happy with my presence, she would finally have a chat with a girl. Just like a good sister she helped me dress, wear makeup, comb my hair ... *Finally a dream come true: a living doll to play with ...* and as if the dress was not enough, she lent me a pair of gold circle earrings and a beautiful bracelet. She is really generous with her things.

Meanwhile, Laura had cooked a tasty dinner, but I I wasn't at all hungry. After taking all my pills I ate very little. After dinner I and Marco (former "shady character") went to the club. I really didn't want to see Remo before work. Max, charming as usual was already there. Marco and I told him what had happened and asked him not to let those two squalid people nor their friends or " suspicious women", namely those women, enter the nightclub alone. That seemed to be my special night. I was angry with Remo, Karen, Lisa and poised to become the most desirable woman of that despicable place, where also decent people with a nice family like Marco worked.

Actually, I was able to do many "tables", I was full of energy and when "I was drinking" with my customers, I practicaly lit up. Whenever a man would choose me, I always asked him why, because there were so many girls more beautiful than me, and the answer was always the same: I was the most joyous, the most lively he had ever met and I was also the most pleasant to be with. I was so delighted to hear that! To get these gentlemen to stay with me I allowed them to touch me and every now and then I also allowed them to kiss me and

sometimes I also touched them back. All I did was out of spite.

I once had a "table" with a wealthy gentleman who held the contract to renovate the premises of a supermarket. After the third drink he wanted at all costs to sleep with me. He actually didn't want to go to bed, he just wanted me to give him a part of my body right there and then, in that booth away from prying eyes. He was totally drunk! He wanted my behind and without any precautions! A real fool! I didn't trust him at all so I very patiently managed to calm him down and I made him come with my hands. He gave me fifty thousand liras for that. He was really pleased to get his pleasure and I was happy to see cash. Immediately after, I started worrying about what I had done and I went to the toilet to wash my hands thoroughly, although he seemed to be a healthy person ... but you never know! After that, I sat with a little old man I didn't like at all; I decided he had to buy a whole bottle if he wanted me to bare with him (In addition to my base salary, I also get a commission based on the the drinks customers buy and the high prices of the bottles they choose are what jack up my percentages by far). *Good girl, you've understood how to make your moves, you're working hard babe*! After a while, he asked me for a job with my mouth. Said, done! I was a little tipsy, but this little game got me another hundred thousand in my pockets. I enjoyed it, for me it's all a game! *Good for you but it's not really just a game, at least for most of us!* Every time Max came by to take orders, I managed to touch him, and customers who were with me never found out I was doing such a thing, and Max enjoyed playing that game so much! I really think he likes me! *What man wouldn't love that!* Now he looks for my touch, and seeks my hand, he tries to touch me too.

When I'n not doing a table with customers I chat with my colleagues: I met a Slovenian girl, Katia, very pretty, we talked mostly of customers, she told me she had a steady one who often takes her out to dinner and who's very generous, gave her many gifts, jewelry for the most. She showed me a beautiful bracelet in gold with three stones, (I don't really understand much about these thing so as far as I know I can't judge whether they are real or fake) flanked by two deep red rounded stones, and the center a stone that resembled a diamond. She told me about her family: She had three little siblings who were studying, two sisters and a brother. Every month she would send money home: her parents used only the essential, the rest was put aside for when she would return. Katia was thinking about opening a small hotel on coming back home. She asked me to double date with her customer and a friend of his; I asked her if we would come back to the club right after dinner but Katia was vague about it so I understood

I couldn't trust her. I'm not afraid that something might happen, but first I want to know whom it happens with, what happens to me and if I agree to what is going to happen; all assessments that I want to do on my own. Wow! *She's getting to be sophisticated!*

August 5, Sunday

(I will not give titles to my days, it's a diary, not a recipe book!)

I'ts finally four o'clock. I was really impatient for closing time! After a short wait, I went home with Marco. I went straight to bed, my little bed near Tiziana's. In the morning they let me rest, I woke up late. Only the three children were home, Marco and Laura had gone out. She worked in an office during the day, at lunchtime she did the cleaning at the club and, in the evening she sometimes took Marco to update the club's accounting work. When her parents were out, Tiziana was the lady of the house, here primary task was to look after her baby brother and restrain the fury of her other brother Simon, who was thirteen years old and a volcano full of energy... he always wanted to fight or play. Tiziana is really a very good little woman of the house, or almost: apart from the cleaning, she cooks, does the washing up, fills washing machines and she competed against her mum in ironing clothes. Tiziana prepared the baby food for her brother Luca in a perfect way, as if he were her son. I was very surprised by her attitude: she had given up her education and hadn't started working so that she could look after her little brother, since her parents were practically never home. She was so dedicated to this mission of hers that she felt really joyful about her life, not in any way depressed. Happy with what she did, she spoke proudly of her work. She was proud of looking after her little brother, instead of complaining all day long about such task that in some way forced her into leading such a limited life. Her behavior was of great value before my eyes. I am really proud to be friends with a young woman, who is only eighteen but turned an onerous and sometimes difficult task, into something so positive and enjoyable, involving others in her joy! And I'm glad that such a beautiful person knows about the job I work, that she doesn't judge me, and that she is indeed convinced that it' just another way as any to make a living. I'm already very fond of her, I'm inside a good family who knows how knows what I do, a family with principles (you can tell by the way the children have been raised), who accept me as I am because they know that you shouldn't only be looking at the label people put on you. I think I'm a nice, clean girl with a positive frame of mind.

At lunch, havig been pushed by my new family, I went to the beach resort. Now that I am a customer, Karen and Lisa can no longer kick me out! Remo was really delighted to see me, he treated me to lunch, then I laid out in the sun and I swam a lot. I wanted to get a good tan! Remo got us a beach umbrella with sunbeds and deck chairs at his own expense just to thank the new family for their hospitality he hadn't been able to offer me himself. I complained about not having the right clothes to work and he asked me, because the next day would be both the mandatory closing day for the resort and his day off, to go shopping with him and to spend a wonderful night together in a hotel. I accepted but I was still very angry about what had happened. I accepted only because I knew I'd buy all sorts of things. Perhaps it will take me a very long time to forgive him! I spent the whole afternoon on my sunbed getting tanned

completely ignoring Remo. I had dinner there because the Marco's home of was too far away and I didn't have a car. My dinner, as usual, went almost entirely to Perlina; I'm no longer interested in food. At 9.40 I headed for the club. It was a little earlier than usual as I had to put make up on. This evening

Laura came by to do the accounting. I saw her from a distance, because I was always very busy. I had four drinks with a gentleman who manufactures pools: a really cool guy, tanned, thin and well dressed. He asked me to sleep with him and we agreed on three hundred thousand lire plus lunch, all for next week: he would come by the club night before the to make arrangements for the following day. Who knows if he will ever come? What's really important It is that had four tables with me. After all my this is my real job, everything else is extra and I never rely on it because it seems to be so uncertain... After I finished the drinks, I went to the sofas with the other girls. There, a very handsome guy dressed casually spoke to me about the fact that he would never pay to talk with someone. Max had come by to remind him of the rules of the club and so he immediately walked away. Soon after I had a table with a guy who offered me a drink. He was a nice young guy who had decided to spend an unusual evening with his friends. He was twenty-four and was really nice. We talked for the whole time: he told me that was attending University, the Faculty of Letters and Science, and his hidden dream was to be a screenwriter. When Max came by to ask if we wanted another drink the guy said yes. For all the second drink we danced. During the third

one, he asked me if I wanted to go to the beach with him. At

this point I told him that I already had a boyfriend, that he owned a beach resort and that I spent all my time with him in the morning. If he wanted to, he could come see me at the club.

When Max came back once again, he immediately stopped drinking with me and went to a table with a Russian girl ... *To tell the truth, such an answer means they have wasted all the drinks they've paid for ... they want girls who tell him only what they want to hear: all fairy tales! ...* I sat down once more and that handsome guy who had been with me before was history, what a pity! I had table with a big blond guy with blue eyes: he told me he owned a bar, he told me where it was and asked if I wanted to go see it. Why not! "If I happen to be in that neighborhood I will definitely come by! " We danced, we made out a bit, but nothing major also because we weren't sitting in a private booth where we could easily hide from prying eyes.

Then it got late for him since he was to open up the bar the next day, so he left; we were almost at closing time anyway.

My drinks are usually sugarless fruit juice or Coke at the most. Any other soft drink or hard liquor drinks don't interest me except bottles of champagne ... a fact of prestige and an economic factor as well! This evening went differently. I

FIRST DAY OF REST

August 6, Monday

By now it was 4, I came home with Marco and went straight to bed. At ten o'clock I woke up: it was late, I was really late. I asked if I could make a phone call. I called to have Remo pick me up and. I wore the nicest dress I had! I'm really happy, after a week of night work I am really tired! Finally a little rest!

At eleven Remo had already arrived at the gate and had rang for me. I went down immediately. He told me that he'd had a hard time finding the house, but eventually, by asking around he finally managed to arrive. I had already told my new family

I would sleep out. We went to another beach resort, we rented a boat and went in the open sea. We did a lot of diving, and maybe I laid out in the sun for too long, I loked like a lobster! We had lunch at a small restaurant and ate a meal all based on

fish. While we were waiting the stores to open, we

had a walk in the woods; then we went round Bellaria's narrow alleys looking for some nice little shop. I stopped in front of almost all the shop windows and I often walked in only just to browse around. Most shops had very high prices. Finally, after a long search we found a little shop with affordable prices. I bought a black, two-piece bathing suit... *Or would you rather say Remo bought it!* ... A short, tight dress, made of black cloth

with flowers, a pink miniskirt and a black top. Obviously Remo

paid for everything. *That's what I meant.* I then convinced him then to "rob" a perfume shop. I bought everything I wanted: a perfume, a bubble bath, a natural sponge, scissors

nail, polish, nail polish remover, etc ... the most amusing thing that happened was that I bought a chap stick. We paid 12,000 liras for it and when we left the shop Remo was totally puzzled an asked me: "But does a chap stick cost so much?" I

answered him "If you get it from a pharmacy you pay 4000 or 5000. " It was as if felt bad about the raw deal he had fallen for! So I immediately smiled broadly and I pointed out that it was a great quality chap stick made by a very good brand. That was enough to get that off his mind and we were both happy once again. I really enjoyed myself! So the afternoon turned into a beautiful evaning. It was dinner time by now and we were both quite tired but despite this we went to dinner in

a cozy restaurant. The dinner was delicious! Here is the final moment: the hotel. *Remo's most awaited moment!* A very nice, clean, small hotel; I felt really at ease there! Our room had air conditioning, and after having set the temperature just right, we made love! When we finished he dozed off. On the contrary

I couldn't sleep and I felt abandoned, used, not considered! … *Yeah right, but what the poor man supposed to do who,*

besides having an unfaithful girlfriend and being generous and kind, was also exhausted by his hard and tiring job … Being accustomed to always staying up late until four in the morning and even later I just couldn't fall asleep. I felt deeply frustrated

by being there, so I locked myself in the bathroom and started

crying … *Deep night club withdrawal symptoms!* … Then,

when I eventually stopped crying, I went back to bed as I felt

very tired, probably because of the exposure to the sun and

I finally fell asleep.

7 August, Tuesday

At 6:30 the alarm clock of the Hotel went off: Remo had to

get up early to go to the beach resort. It was really hard to wake up for me, now I used to stay awake at night and go to bed at that hour. He suggested that I stay there a while longer

there but then I did not know how to get home, so I decided to

go back with him. We had breakfast together at a bar near the resort, I had a cappuccino and croissant, while Remo had coffee and croissant stuffed with custard, he's really fond of them! Then he went to work, I took my time and decided to I lay in the sun some more, on the sunbed in front of the

sea. At about 10:30 the heat became unbearable, I went by Remo to get ice cream and then I went at home; and to get there I had a long walk, I want a car! Tiziana let me in. I was really tired, so I fell asleep. When I sleep, I'm used to

total silence, but this place is too noisy for me to sleep during the day. So I got into the habit of using the wax caps

to be able to get to sleep. I woke up in the afternoon

and I really wished there would be an extremey sunny summer that year so that Remo could benefit from the good weather and keep his job all summer long. But unfortunately the two daughters of the owner of the resort, Karen and Lisa, who had behaved unjustly with me would benefit from the good weather too. Well, it doesn't matter! ... *You want me to buy that it was thanks to your prayers that they had great weather all summer long? It is true that almost no one prays for good weather conditions so maybe you got good results just for that ...* In the late afternoon everyone was back home. Tiziana and I decided to go out. After Tiziana placed Luca on the stroller, we had a nice walk around the city. She knew that town real well so we saw the most beautiful places: hidden squares, aincient steps, narrow streets and shaded porches. As we were enjoying our stroll we ran into a friend of hers: a really hansome guy who was her same age, he had green eyes, dark blond hair, a lean body and his name was Dario. Tiziana introduced me as her a friend of hers. They chatted a bit, but tried to keep me out of their things: she was really open to me but a little shy at the same time, perhaps there's something going on between them and she doesn't want to show it. Maybe Tiziana will tell me when she's ready. Actually, we're becoming real friends. *But I thought you were sisters by now ...* Yup! Shell'tell me! Anyway, I did feel good with the two of them. Tiziana has the gift to put me at ease, she's really an exquisite girl! I seem to be living in another world; everybody is so nice to me here, everybody is so real, it's just fine! ... *You can feel good anywhere, in any city, just choose the right people who won't judge you, but would rather get to know you. After all, we can not be all the same, but when we run into someone different from us we sometimes cannot accept it. Choosing people more similar to us makes us feel more comfortable, that way we don't have to face our prejudice! ...*

After our walk we went back home, because Tiziana wanted to iron some clothes. I got ready for work, Laura wanted to comb my hair, Tiziana lent me a nice pair of earrings. I went to dinner with Remo. We stayed together for a while, we chatted until 10 when I started work at the night club. It looked like it was going to be a real boring evening; Tuesday was expected to be rather still but instead I have always worked well on Tuesdays. Maybe it's the way Max introduces me to customers that made them choose me ... who knows what sort of idea they get about me. First, I had a table with a man who kept on rambling about his problems with his wife, I know that this guy drinks too much ... I tried to make him forget about his sad thoughts for a while, but sometimes he seemed as if he wasn't listening to me and so he missed the meaning of my words ... *who knows maybe he was drunk or what you were talking about was really boring, or perhaps more than boring, you swang from one topic to another at the speed of light so that the poor man was lost at times ...* Then I did other tables that didn't last that long with various men who were really curious about my life. I never thought that what I had done that far was that interesting ... *Why haven't you realized yet that men who hang out at nightclubs, as well as many other men, just want to take you to bed? Perhaps the difference is that the ones who go to nightclubs are willing to pay to achieve their goal! ...* It was one in the morning when the client I was with almost caught me looking at another man with a stunned expression. That nice guy who had talked to me days before had entered the club. I could not believe it! Not only he was back, but he also wanted to offer me a drink. He was even more handsome and charming than the first time. He was dressed really elegant: gray pants, black shirt, dark gray jacket. No tie, too bad! I like men dressed in elegant suits! ... *Oh really? ...* He smelled really good, and for the occasion had grown a goatee. Wow, he was really a hunk! Hot Stuff ! With a goatee he was really a dream! Yes and He wanted to sit on the most visible and lit sofa and in the club: I wasn't used to it and it was almost an event for me! We immediately both felt the need to get to know one another better, break down the barriers that separated us, to share thr most intimate things! But how could we do that in just twenty minutes of conversation? The more we talked, the more I liked him and I thought his name Rico suited him just perfectly. He bombarded me with questions and the more I answered him, the more questions he would ask me; I saw him getting more and more involved, as if he was actually interested in me! Instead, he practically didn't tell me anything about himself. Who knows maybe I was wrong? I felt great with him! When Max came to say that the time had expired, he wanted to offer me another drink. So we chatted a bit longer. The longer I was with Rico, the more he itrigued me. At the end of the second table he left saying he would be back another day to see me again. I was very upset when left! I immediately missed his reassuring presence. Yes, he gave a sense of security! ... *You'd be reassured by the presence of an iguana, but fortunately most people are like you, perhaps even worse: What*

would people do to aviod being alone! ... The evening was over, there was no one left in the club so we closed early.

August 8, Wednesday

Marco had left eary, so Max, at this late hour, offered to take me home. Maybe he wanted to hit on me? We first took the other girls of club home and then he took me home. He wanted to chat a bit, but he didn't try anything; too bad! ... *Stay calm, he's only waiting for the right moment, when he hits on you and won't miss!* ... I found the front door open, then I rang at Marco's apartment and I didn't have the keys because I always come back home with him in the morning. Nobody came to open the door and I was so sleepy that I fell asleep sitting on the door threshold! At six o'clock Laura who was really worried, opened the door and found me lying on the on the cold marble feeling a little numb! She was really sorry she hadn't heard me when I rang, but I couldn't just wake them all up! I went to bed and I slept soundly until eleven. I couldn't believe it, a procession of apologies began immediately for not having heard the doorbell. The family decided to give me a set of keys: the only keys available were Tiziana's who wasn't leading such a glamorous nightlife anyway, linked as she was to her little brother, she

hardly ever left her home. I had my breakfast: coffee and milk. I started to read a book that I had started back in Rome: a very interesting esoteric story. After a shower, for lunch, the family dragged me to a very important event for all of them: the wedding anniversary of their grandparents on Laura's side of the family. Tiziana's grandparents live in a nice house with a garden. Fortunately, it's a quiet area. Here, as allover Bellaria, I must say that you can leave your car unlocked and no one will steal anything. Beautiful! It didn't take us long to get there. I was introduced as a very dear friend of Tiziana's: I was the only friend among close relatives, I felt honored for so much consideration ... *But hadn't you ever been invited to a ceremony? Cinderella!* I was just fine: their grandparents' house is very cool! They are very old but completely autonomous, in any sense: they had done their shopping for the party and cooked too. They also managed to carry out all the paperwork that Laura would often hand them because they had more time on their hands being freer from a real daily routine. My "new family" was used to my way of eating so they defended me: no one forced me in any way to eat more than I was used to, but I must say I ate some including the delicious Millefoglie cake, grandma's masterpiece. In the afternoon after lunch, I and my new family hit the road to give the grandparents a chance to rest. I'm glad I finally seem to have found my ideal family, a family like I've always wanted: one for all and all for one, united, loving, numerous. *Yup, but it's a shame is not your family!* We, the children and the others went to the beach directly from the party because Laura and Marco had to do the cleaning at club, where we had everything available to us: a beach umbrella for the children, a table, chairs etc. and especially ice cream at will for all! All this thanks to Remo who felt guilty over what I had to undergo (eviction plus all the various slanderous charges): he felt he was indebted to them for their hospitality. There on the beach, while Simone was playing in the sand building prisons for crabs, I told Tiziana about meeting Rico … after all she was a sister to me and she was quite a positive little person. I must say that, as I expected, Tiziana felt sincerely my emotions, and shared them as only a sister can! The afternoon went by in a blink of an eye! Laura prepared dinner while her daughter looked after her little brother as she always does. After dinner, with Marco, we went to the club and he gave me the third degree: he wanted to know what I and Enrico had talked about. I was totally transparent, I told him the truth: He had tried to hit on me for a while. Marco told me that Rico was not his real name but Enrico was. He was a policeman and

I had to be careful about what I talked about when I was with him. Then he also said Rico posed as singles and so he had lied to me: not only he was married, but he actually had two young children. For me it was a low blow! But I didn't want to show it to Marco and I tried to play cool … *Your facial expression was probably shouting "tragedy". But then in the end, didn't you have a boyfriend yourself? …* I immediately changed the topic. I couldn't think about it there and then … I would think about that later on: after this bad piece of news the evening looked like it was going to last forever! I arrived at the club and I tried to fool around with Max so that I wouldn't think about Rico (or Enrico as I discovered his name was). Max seemed a bit more interested in me, or maybe it was what I was hoping for as when one door closes, another one opens … *Honey, in your case a hotel full of doors wouldn't be enough! …* I just couldn't stop thinking about Rico, my brain was smoking, what could I do? Nothing! After all I did have a boyfriend: I've never had so many suitors, but were they serious or had I imagined them all? I just couldn't understand anything anymore … *As if you did before! …* there was total chaos in my mind! When they put the usual disco music on I danced like crazy just to get tired and get thoughts off my mind, and that gave me unexpected positive results: customers, who were quite impressed by so much energy, chose me more than usual. So, by spending time talking to them the night flew away more quickly. Among the many custmers I had conversations with, a gentleman who owned of a textile shop and home textiles really impressed me; I immediately asked him if he sold double sheets of black silk. He said yes! Wow! So, speaking about this and that, my interest in material things came out so he proposed an exchange: an afternoon with him in exchange for black silk sheets of the commercial value of 350 / 400,000 lire. Of course I very happily accepted, also because that way he would stay with me and have more drinks: I was just working, and everything else would be about the future. I began to be a bit skeptical when he told me he wouldn't be around for about a week for work reasons so if I wanted to change my mind, I had all the time I wanted to think about it. It was already 2 the morning. I couldn't wait to get home and forget about Rico. Max had offered to take me home because Marco had to leave early because he felt sick, this time we would be alone: the bouncer was taking the other girls home; I enjoyed his company and he really attacted me, like a forbidden fruit. I had investigated on him: Max was married to a rich woman: he had opened a small supermarket. He really didn't love her, but he couldn't give up the luxury he was accustomed to. Then, to get her to marry him he had to bite quite a few bullets, especially having to endure her stepfather that often reminded him that without this new family he wouldn't have been able to get anything out of life. Max, almost out of revenge went with all the women that interested him: he was full of stories. But maybe they were just rumors ... *You should always listen to popular rumors, there is always a bit of truth in gossip!*

August 9, Thursday

At four, with the excuse that he had to close the club, we stayed to chat for a while: he told me of his passion

for billiards. He said that at the level he plays, he participated in various competitions that he often won, and that one day, if I want, I can go to his house to see his awards ... *Yes, his private collection of butterflies!* ... He then confirmed the rumor of his insignificant wife, saying that now their marriage is practically over. They have no children. However, he denied rumors of having any other girls ... *So it is true that you believe that donkeys fly! ...*We chatted until five. Then Max

came over and kissed me, he was very tender! Then this

tenderness became more and more intense mutual attraction and his hands looked for my skin, and in a moment we were embraced without clothes and when I was at the height of excitement he very calmly put on a condom.

That cooled me off a bit! I thought he hadn't let himself go the same way I had done with him. But seeing that was even more of a man than Remo, passion took hold of me once more, but it was not for this feature I hadn't known about until then that Max had attracted me from the first time I saw him: he had a strange charm, the mystery man in the night! We made love, it was very nice, very passionate, I abandoned myself almost entirely to this stranger who knew really how to treat a woman in bed. Maybe it was true that he'd been with many women, but they made him what he was they were all welcome ...

We often love someone for one of their particular characteristics, but when we find out what events arose this particular gift

we almost don't like it anymore the most and so becomes the very reason why we hate them! I felt like I was back in paradise, a

completely physical paradise! But how could I have let my yet not well defined feelings for Rico fade away, a sentiment that surely could not bloom for Max! I knew his story, he had been honest ... and he knew mine, there couldn't be a future

and perhaps not even a present between us. Only an interlude of intense pleasure. Finally, I was an adult and as only men are able to do, I can separate love and sex from work. I could afford to behave any way I chose to and my new family wouldn't judge me, instead try'd try to understand ... *Sure understand a boyfriend, your work, the lover, the new love ... all together it wasn't so complicated to swallow especially if you were completely devoid of morality! Or maybe they didn't understand anything and had given up even trying to!* ... I enjoyed this parenthesis a lot and I envisioned several others

in my brain which had gone off the deep end! ... *Fortunately*

that you admitted that you have a brain that flies on its own

in the clouds! ... Max asked me to say nothing about what had just happened and he would do the same. It seemed a good idea. So I was back home, all satisfied by pleasure ... he had fulfilled a small part of me. I slept like a log until noon .. what's the hurry anyway? I really didn't want to go to the beach to be with Remo. I also didn't care for any lunch, I already felt full. The rest of the family would not give up lunch for the world and Tiziana convinced me to go to the beach to see Remo while she was doing the washing up... *Poor puppy ... all alone!* ... but he wasn't there, he had gone to run a few errands. Too bad for him, or perhaps much better for me, he wouldn't have had the opportunity to realize that there was something different in me: perhaps I was starting to be aware of the fact that I might be nymphomaniac! ... *who doesn't like to make love, and most of the ones who've had more experiences are keen on having as many as possible ...* I like to make love and I also like many men, not everyone of them, but many, just maybe I care about their sexuality which I now live in a much freeer and open way than I did before. I was soaking up the sun on my sunbed when Remo showed up with an ice cream. I liked the surprise very much! not so much him showing up but I enjoyed the icicle anyway. He didn't look like he was aware of anything and I thought it was better that way ... *Just like the old proverb goes: "If the eye does not see, the heart does not grieve!" We often cling to this with all our soulpretending nothing really happened! Convenient isn't it? A bit "sad, but don't people actually do that?!*

I cannot manage to feel any guilt, maybe if I had neglected

Remo, making him sad and unhappy, only then perhaps!

But he was fine and unaware of anything, I was happier that way and that little remorse of mine resulted in me being nicer to him. We had a swim together. Then he went back

to work and I went back on my sunbed in the sun. I never laid out in the sun so much, not even when I was a child! I hung out a bit with him at the bar, then I went back home. Tiziana helped me out in my usual preparation for the evening. I didn't say anything about what had happened between Max and me, maybe I felt awkward to talk about something that didn't involve any feelings at all, but only my senses. I wonder if she would understand as only a real sister could... just to be on the safe side, the fear of being judged negatively by someone who I felt like a sister to me was too strong, so I kept this secret in my little heart ... she was too important for me to lose over such a petty incident. Also because that far, I had always mixed up feelings and sex, or work and sex; then how could I explain that new attitude of mine that was inexplicable also for me? I went to work with Marco as usual and he hit on me as well. A shock to me! Had he been drinking? I was petrified ... *Wake up! They all want the same thing ... They are men ...* I managed to play cool so he stopped, maybe he didn't know what to do! ... *Maybe he knew what he was doing and hoped that you wouldn't know how to react ... maybe he saw a little uncertainty in your sexual future! ...* When we arrived at the club I drank a gin and tonic to recover from my shock, the only alcoholic beverage I like apart from champagne. I got back on track pretending nothing had happened. I had to remove this unpleasant fact from my mind! I did a table with a gentleman who sold swimming pools. He looked familiar to me. I felt like I had already met him before. He asked me to spend the following afternoon with him, for 250,000 lire, lunch included. I accepted, an extra is always welcome and he's a handsome man, lean body, blond with blue eyes, who knows why he needs to pay for women? Perhaps he cannot get excited? Well, that's his business anyway; I'm having a trip tomorrow and I'll enjoy myself a lot. We agreed to meet up at 1 p.m. in a small square. Yes ... I could do with some extra cash although I never spend any money: I was always at home or at the resort where I never paid for anything.

For my salary at the club I'd have to wait fifteen days to go by and I think that I'll send the whole paycheck home anyway. That way, they can at least pay off one or more of their overdue installments, depending on how much I can make. The very moment we made agreements this man left. Maybe I was too quick in saying say yes to him. I really should play harder to get a bit more. Next time I'll be smarter. After that, I had several juices with men I didn't know.

August 10, Friday

I got back home together with Marco. He didn't do anything strange, as if nothing had happened, Much better this way!

Maybe he was just pretending because he saw he wasn't getting anywhere. During the return trip I told him about the invitation to lunch I had received and his comment was "Everything okay, but next time, have them take you to dinner!". When we got home I immediately went to sleep. I woke up at ten, perhaps because of the emotion of the date I was going to have. Actually, I have to say that I was a bit scared to spend the whole afternoon with a stranger. I tried not to think about it. I chatted for a couple of hours with Tiziana and I thought to myself that afternoons, as long as they migh seem to me, had a well defined length. So I managed to calm down. I gave out instructions: if Remo had phoned they were to say that I was having

a walk around town. I wore a denim mini-skirt, a low-cut T-shirt with colorful flowers, a pair of sandals and a small hand bag that matched the skirt. All pretty and wearing daytime makeup. I arrived early as my usual. After a while, he showed up too. His name was Luca, had a beautiful car, a brand new blue Opel Calibra. When he opened the door, I noticed that the door was like the ones of luxury sports cars have, where only the glass sticks out. After he started his sports car we took off towards the hotel that would host us. However, we took a very busy country road. So Luca, as if he were race car driver, passed all the cars that were in front of us risking both for the high speed and for the dangers that a narrow street can hide. I enjoyed that a lot as I was completely unconscious of what could have happened; he managed to go even at 200 km per hour. It was a great feeling! Finally We arrived at our destination. It was a third-rate hotel, more like a family hotel ... *Yea, a family by-the-hour-fleabag!* ... He asked for a room for

the afternoon, we were asked to leave our ID cards at the reception and then we went upstairs. We got into the room: he took a shower, I hadn't sweated during our little journey, especially with the air of the two open windows flowing in would have been difficult. Then he came in the bedroom was all naked! All muscular and lean! He approached the bed and asked to do a striptease for him. I obeyed, while

Luca was lying on the bed in my place. I will was

good, because he got all excited immediately! He did not want to use a condom and I hadn't brought anything with me anyway. He swore he would come out of me, but unfortunately it was just a lie: in a moment he had me all wet! So I ran to the bathroom to rinse with heaps of soap, hoping nothing had happened; I wasn't on the pill and so I could get very well get

pregnant. This made me a bit angry, not I could no longer trust this man. He than took me to lunch. On the way back there was always a little traffic that he passed brilliantly overtaking other cars, creating dangerous situations! That reckless man! I don't like him, all full of himself without any consideration for others!

We stopped at a restaurant on the way back. We had prosciutto and melon and it was the first time I ate with a little more appetite than usual compared to the last periods. We also ate other things, all delicious. Then, after lunch, he took me back where we initially met up. During lunch he told me: "What will you answer if you are asked you how it was?" And I didn't knew how to answer him. And then Luca went on saying: "Don't say anything!" So, just to have a conversation I asked him the same question: "And what will you say if you are asked how I was? " and he replied:" I will tell them that you're a great slut! "I was about to get angry when then he said: "That way you'll work more!" Well, I hadn't thought about that, so I had a good laugh. When he dropped me off at the liitle square I was overjoyed to have earned my 250,000 liras I finally had some my money for myself so I went shopping around and bought a

few little things: a nice little black dress for work and black open summer heels, to be even more attractive. At home all my new family was interested to know how my date had turned out and I told them the witty exchange of lines I had at lunch and they laughed too. However, I skipped the part where

I didn't take any precautions; I did not want to be judged

too naive. *Surely you're not very good at protecting yourself considering where you live, surrounded by white clouds ... there is no need to do that!* As always, they had dinner, but I had no appetite so I spent more time getting ready: I put

on the new dress with open shoes. After, I went to the club with Marco. Tonight I did a table with a man who works for the State railways. A simple man, a little overweight, not so handsome, wearing worn out clothes. He fell in love with me from the first moment he sat next to me, and wanted at all costs to get engaged with me and that we should get married. He couldn't grasp the situation ... If only he had been handsome and attractive or rich and educated .... but he was non of the above! He said that by being with him, I'd earn free trips with the railways throughout Italy. I felt that it was just too little for me. But, mindful of my primary duty in my job of entertaining customers, I spoke with him about many things having him believe that I actually wanted to know him better in the future. It wasn't a total lie ... actually I'm quite a curious girl. Maybe I let him believe a little more than what I was willing to with him. We had at least four or five tables. That's all money in my pockets. I also did a table with a tall blonde a bit abundant guy, who was really pleasant. In fact, he wasn't that bad ... his eyes were blue and his name was Giorgio ... But I think I had already met him. It was that guy at the bar, what who invited me to have breakfast with him a few days before. He was very forthcoming. He seemed to feel at ease with me. I, unlike my colleagues, when someone put his hands on me I stood there like a toy in the hands of a child. Certainly, no one I didn't allow them to exaggerate without paying an extra. This did not seem a guy willing to pay for an extra. He looked like a nice guy, maybe a little shy ... he just wanted to get engaged

and start a family. *That makes two!* By mid-night I had a big surprise: Remo showed up together with our mutual friend Joe. He offered me a couple of drinks and we chatted a bit. Joe

did two tables with another girl. Then we said goodbye.

This was a particularly surprising day! Old customers I had the first night started to come back: The old man of the bottle also came back and wanted me to give him the same service like the last time. It seems as if he liked it! I didn't feel like doing it at that moment because I wasn't desperate enough to accept anything for lack of tables. I was no longer a beginner! It was a happy moment, I was working very much so I could choose what to do, when and with whom. So I was able to make him pay for four drinks, but at the fourth one I think he understood that I had no plans to offer him the same treatment as the last time. So, he then decided to jack up his offer to two hundred,

three hundred thousand but I decided not to give in.

Starting from today, Friday, there was a new attraction: a few

new, beautiful girls did a striptease show. So at the time of the show I convinced him, that old man, to go on the sofas in front of the dance floor dance to enjoy it better. That way my client would keep his hands more in their place! It was a good show in the end: the girls were good, perhaps real dancers. Among them was a black girl lean, tall, slim with blue eyes. She was also very much in demand because girls doing the shows are usually chosen much more than us normal girls, although their tables are more expensive than ours. She was a good girl, really very nice.

August 11, Saturday

Marco did not feel very well, so he left way before, so Max would take me back home. We had to take many of the other girls home including the beautiful black girl named Shanthal. She was worried because she had drunk a bit too much and her, rich, boyfriend from a good family was waiting for her at the hotel and he realy didn't want her to do this work, let alone seeing her drunk. On the other hand, he gave her no concrete financial help. So she felt compelled to work here and usually, whenever she met up with her boyfriend, he would beat her. We accompanied her with Max that walked her into the hotel because she couldn't walk standing straight. Then, he took me me to Marco's house. During the journey he complained saying he just couln't believe that Marco had felt sick once again. And he asked me, as I slept at his house, to investigate and let him know the truth. I agreed, but only to make him happy. I didn't care about their diatribes. And surely I could not go against those who hosted me and fed me: my new family. This time having the keys I didn't ring at the door. I went to bed and fell asleep. When I woke up I decided to go see Remo at the beach resort. It was about noon so he invited me to stay for lunch: He prepared very good meatballs, with a little salad. After that, to work out that food, I decided to go back home on foot. Marco's car had broken down. I was somewhat sorry for that so I tried to remember wheter among my customers there was a mechanic, so I would ask him to fix it as if it were mine, giving my performance that basically did not cost me much in return. Yup, often these men, like Luca the guy who sold swimming pools, come immediately when they have sex, so I didn't even have to be together with them for too long. In the afternoon I went for a long walk with Tiziana who, as usual brought her little brother Luca with us. And before you know it, it was time to get ready to go to work again. Laura and Tiziana helped me comb my hair and make me pretty as usual. We went to the club with Marco in a car borrowed from a friend of his. It looked like it would be quite a busy evening. At weekends, there were many more men at the club, so the girls who did not work during the week made up for it in the weekend. The first customer was a gentleman who owned a gas station, I'd never done a table with him before. He was very pleasant and friendly and he had never put his hands on me. We chatted a bit about my work. He was very interested. I replied vaguely. A rule of the nightclub was that we girls do not tell anything about our job. He asked me if I sometimes wanted to spend some time at his gas station and maybe have my car washed for free. I didn't say no, I thought I could perhaps take Marco's or Remo's car there to get fixed if they needed. This evening Marco had felt ill once again. So Max was very restless, he had to do twice the work: bartender and purveyor of clients. But, fortunately the bouncer was also there to help out at the end of the night to take some girls back home. But it was not enough, Max was convinced that Marco pretended to be sick, because he didn't want to work. I personally had no reason to doubt of his illness, but I did not care to pry into the business of others, I wanted to stay out of it! A group of ten young boys came to the club.

They wanted to celebrate the birthday of one of them. So they rented Chantal for a private striptease for him. And they also got a few other girls to perk up the evening. I was a member of their group as well. They ordered champagne. So I did at least ten tables with them. They were quite wealthy guys. They were also handsome. It turned out that with their girlfriends from good families they did not want to do any special things. So they came to the club to let off some steam. They did not want to do anything at all with us at the club and they wanted us to go with them to their hotel for an orgy. I had never seen them before so I didn't trust them. With the excuse to go to the bathroom, I asked Max if he knew them. He replied that they were not regulars, but they wanted to pay us the end of the evening in advance and in cash. I had never had an orgy before and I really didn't want to start that night and bargain with

untrusted and unknown people. I had a hard time dropping them because some of the girls who had done only few tables during the week thought it would be convenient to have the evening paid in full and they did not want me to abandon them. They, too were frightened and wanted my support. I stayed at the club telling the guy who was with me that alone we could do everything he wanted, but with his friends I didn't feel at

ease and that he could come back to see me whenever he wanted. I did a few more table and then a curious thing happened.

August 12, Sunday

At about two o'clock Rico, the policeman, came to the club and asked Max if he could take me home. Max made me go into a dressing room and told me that someone had come to pick me up. This dressing room, the same one as I had my job interview in, had two entrances: one led into the club, the other was a second entrance designed specifically to let girls leave the club without customers or coworkers seeing it. I was very curious to know who had come to pick me up and I was also a bit worried! Why Max was so sure I wanted to go with this person? I could not believe it was him. And he had managed to get me out early. He had me get into his car, a blue station wagon. Here we

headed towards the woods. The ride was almost magical with the moon illuminating our path. Rico found a secluded parking lot as if he knew that area really well. In fact, he told me that

was often there on patrol. I asked him if there was any danger that someone might come to disturb us. He showed me his badge and then the gun that he immediately hid under his seat. He would protect me. Thus reassured, I let myself go. He put on some audio cassette. How could he know? All my favorite romantic songs. We had the same taste. It was beautiful and being next to him made me want to surrender to anything he would ask me. We chatted for two long hours. He eventually approached me, took my face in his hands and started to kiss me. They were tender and passionate kisses. I really wanted him, but I did not want him to think I was an easy girl so I suggested to have swim in the sea ... *Well, he certainly never thought you were an easy girl ... in fact you weren't working in a nightclub and you had never walked out with a customer! Another clever guy in your life! How lucky! Or perhaps he had hit his head real hard! ...* The water was warm, we had no swimming suits and we couldn't get our clothes wet so we decided to swim naked. I was so embarrased of him and couldn't understand why. Suddenly Rico asked me: "Is it true that you sleep around with everyone?" And I answered: "No, but who told you that? I might have slept with one person at the most, but that's all". He insisted almost giving me the third degree to know why I hadn't found a regular job and why I was forced to do this. I explained that I had fun. He wanted to see me working a normal job as soon as possible. I explained that I had tried a normal job, but I was not able to find anything that would allow me to help my parents pay their debts back. I was doing this instead and it was a very lucrative job. At one point he calmed down or something like that: He hugged me real tight and started kissing me ... the desire to make love took over the both of us. He had me lie down on the sand and very gently, with passion, he finally possessed me. It was the first time that I was loved on the sand. We did it in my favorite position (I below, above him) and that was also his. We didn't use any protection. I let myself go completely, I really relaxed, I was able to have an orgasm, and for me it is very difficult. However, he did not come himself. Right after that we rinsed the sand off into the sea and dried at best; we returned to the car where he started kissing me again, we got excited once again and so we started making love. We actually have the same tastes! We were back in my favorite position! I felt like I was in heaven! That seemed to guess what I liked and it was natural for him to behave that way. Eventually, he came but out of me.

It was now past 6:30 and he said he had to go back to work, then we slowly got ourselves dressed and then he drove me home. I had told him that I felt a little overweight before so he took my face in his hands he gave me a tender kiss and mocking me he said: "See you soon, my little fatso!" I easily got inside the building with my house keys. In the apartment they were all asleep. I didn't have a shower right away ... I wanted to keep the scent of Rico's skin on my body for a while longer, I liked it a lot. At lunch time I got a call from Joe who was very angry.

This time I woke up late. My new family was not at home. Joe accused me of not being at home in the morning. Actually, I had plunged into a deep sleep sweetened by Rico's scent. I hadnt slept so well in a long time. Since I slept with earplugs I mustn't have heard the intercom nor the telephone ring until I I woke up and so I answered at approximately one thirty. Joe claimed he phoned and rang me at the same time and that I can't have been there, otherwise I would have woken up. It's not that I wasn't there, really ... I was sleeping like a log and I didn't hear a thing! The fact is that he tried to make trouble between me and Remo. So I had to go to the resort and talk to both. Bottom line, Joe didn't believe me and he thought that I had been out with a customer doing who knows what ... Remo believed me though. The fact is dramatic because I was there indeed! Anyway, if Joe didn't believe me I really wouldn't care that much. In the afternoon, I took a walk with Joe and he asked me if I had been with someone else. I told him the truth, that I had been out a few days before with a guy who sells pools. Joe asked me not to say anything to Remo: he wanted to protect his friend from the truth. He didn't care if I did this for work, what was important to him was that Remo wouldn't know about it. I told him not to worry, that I wasn't not going to tell him. Then he asked me if I used condoms and I had to I confess that I didn't, so he yelled at me and gave me a pep talk you give to someone as helpless as I am! Deep down inside of him he really cared for me, I was his favorite buddy and so he gave me a packet of condoms, saying that I absolutely had to use them. After all this fuss I made up with Remo and Joe and they believed me. All's well what ends well! *Crazy stuff, you have to*

justify your behaviour with two men who both want you, and both justify what you do ... do you realize that? Anyway

I got a bad rap for half a day. Today Marco didn't come to work, maybe he was really ill, I don't think he can fake an inexisting illness for more than more days in a row and this morning, he must have gone to be examined with his whole family

otherwise they would have answered to Joe's calls. Max was ever more angry with Marco. He and I always kept on

playing, so I managed to ease his mind a little. Every so often when he passed by, I touched him and he also did the same. Even though I had told Joe had reported that I had slept with the guy who sells pools, I had actually failed to tell him more compromising things, that I'd had sex with Max and that it had been beautiful, I'd had a love date with Rico and I had felt magnificently well. He surely would have neither understood nor tolerated these facts. Having sex for money was something Joe was able to grasp and approve of. Joe had many friends who did this, which suits many girl strippers he knew well. So, he was used to people selling their body for money. Instead parallel love stories, especially if a close friend is directly involved, was something he couldn't handle easily. I had a few more tables with different men. At about three o'clock I saw Rico coming, I would have never expected him to show up! Max was almost upset about that ... too bad for him! Rico took me back to pinewood once again and we talked all night. Or rather almost ... we talked a lot and we made love too. It was the the first time a man made me come so many times. I lost count. I was really fine! Making love to Rico is fantastic. We seem to just two parts of a puzzle that fit together perfectly. He also said he was very surprised that he had found girl who had made him lose his mind. And he had met a whole lot of different girls. Unfortunately, the second part of the night was too short. Perhaps, time flew fast because we were both really at ease! It was already dawn, so reluctantly Rico drove me back at Marco's. As I got out of the car he said: "Be a goog girl now!" And I replied: " Of course! " But deep down inside, I knew I couldn't keep my word. It wasn't my fault I was made that way! *Like what? Completely out of the box trapped inside your need of infinite love! ...*

August 13, Monday

Today was a day off for me and Remo just like every Monday. I was so happy of the night before that I just couldn't fall asleep so late in the morning I called Remo to have him be pick me up. Of course I felt a little guilty, but I was also very happy. Basically I felt as I wasn't neglecting Remo. He took me out for lunch to a typical restaurant of the place. A family owned restaurant. But my heart was racing at 3000 rpm. and my thoughts were all for Rico, I didn't eat much so Remo started to worry, I had him believe that it was the excitement of being together at last. *This might seem cruel! But since I know her, I can that such behaviour is part how she atually is: a totally out of the ordinary woman not capale to be seen for what she really is, as she is scared of the opinions of others. Pretty much like all of us who we become what others expect to see, and we also support their opinion without our say in order not to be judged!* As usual in the afternoon we did a bit of shopping and, knowing how much I loved beauty items Remo made me a very nice and useful gift: a large, famous brand cosmetic bag, complete with everything. Wow! So I would be able to wear make up a thousand times better and be even more beautiful. He also bought a very nice colored dress. Well, Remo is actually really sweet! This time with the excuse of being a bit sweaty and that I should wear my new dress, he brought me to the hotel early in the afternoon. Surprise! Remo had bought a lingerie set and a pair of high heels and I said, "While I take a shower, try on the lingerie with the shoes and the dress so we can see how you

49

look! "I felt both embarrassed and a little excited at the same time! Did he have great desire for me? *Oh yes men have a fixed mind!* Who knows, maybe trying on the dress, wearing the lingerie, taking a shower, maybe ... they were all pretexts. Maybe He was very excited and wanted to make love to me and he just couldn't wait after dinner as usual. When He came out of the shower you could see he was already very excited. So he sat on the bed and told me to take a few steps to see how I was the new dress. Then he asked me to do a little striptease for him. I'm a bit shy so I undressed quite slowly. I was still in my bra, thong panties and shoes with heels and waited for him to make the first move. Immediately he embraced me and the towel that covered his abdomen dropped. He lowered the straps of my bra and kissed my nipples. Then he laid on the bed and after having taken my panties off we made love. Strangely enough, he wanted me to keep my heels on. Who knows ... maybe they got him very excited! His performance was very long as usual. Perhaps his surprise had excited me too so I came three times myself. He only once, at the end. And got me all wet across my belly. So while he was resting in bed watching TV, I took a shower and then we went to dinner. I wore his lingerie, the new dress, but my old shoes which were a bit more comfortable. At dinner I was very hungry so I made Remo happy and I ate a lot more than my usual. After dinner we went on the beach to have a drink. Then, being both rather tired we went back to the hotel, and straight to bed.

August 14, Tuesday

As usual, we woke up at dawn, 6:30. Remo was concerned about the fact that Marco's car was broken and so he lent me his own. We had breakfast together at the usual little bar, and I took him to the resort where he worked. In fact, I had slept all night so I wasn't sleepy at all and when I got home I started to chat with Tiziana telling her about Remo and his gifts. I avoided to tell her about the lingerie set because I was ashamed about it! Then I also told her about Rico without specifying what we had done for the last two nights. We only had petty talk. I expressed my concerns about not knowing what to do if I had been forced to choose between Remo and Rico. As a wise sister, Tiziana suggested that I should not decide now and furthermore, Rico was already married and had children. "Live it as a fun experience" she told me. Now I really don't feel like making any important decisions! *Nobody asked you to make any! But in your life it's as if you followed a truth of justice that belongs to you only ... rather incomprehensible for most of us, unfortunately ...* The whole little family gathered for lunch at home, I ate very little. After all I'd eaten so much the night before and I'd also had breakfast. In afternoon I did not want to go out so I stayed home reading a good book. At the club as usual, being tuesday we weren't expecting a big rush. Fortunately, the night went by the same. I did some table with a few funny men ... none noteworthy, all short tables. At least I did my share! The nightclub usually closed at five but in the days when there was no work it could close earlier. Fortunately tonight It closed at three-thirty. Too bad that I didn't see Rico! Together with Marco, we took some of the girls

home. Or rather in the apartments that the owner of the club rented them. During the journey Marco asked the girls if Max had behaved propery with them. All of them said yes. After we dropped off the girls he also asked me so many questions as he usually did usual. I was a tomb! I'm really improving!

It's easy to say nothing about something that we hide to everyone! Who knows, perhaps in part also to ourselves ...

August 15, Wednesday

Marco and I got home aand went to sleep. Today is August and Remo has a lot of work to do. At the resort they take advantage of the

51

holidays to earn some extra money. My little family asked me to go with them to their grandparents' for lunch to celebrate Ferragosto. I was very glad for their invitation, I am always very at ease when I'm with them. Lunch was very

tasty. They, again, had cooked all by themselves. We stayed there only until lunch was over. The Grandparents are used to taking a nap in the afternoon and when we came back home we rested a bit too. Taking advantage of the holiday and of the fact that they were all home, Laura and Tiziana started cleaning the house inside out. I helped them even though they didn't want me to, it seemed really bad just staying there doing nothing while they were shining up the house. After dinner, I got dressed up and went to the club with Marco. We arrived a little early because today is finally payday. I had a wonderful surprise! I expected a salary of one million five hundred thousand liras instead I got two million three hundred fifty thousand liras ... WOW! It must have been all the bottles, which are paid separately. I'm happy! I've never seen so much money. I asked Marco if I could get them at the end of the evening. He agreed. I was a bit worried that someone might take them

from me. Since I was very happy with the result I was even perkier than usual. I started working right away. That client worked for the railways and wanted at all costs and get engaged and marry me came back. We did at least a dozen tables. We talked a lot while he was trying to touch me, but I managed to defend myself thanks to the fact that he had serious intentions. After, he had to leave but he promised me he would soon return to see me and I saw myself forced to at least to give him a kiss. Then I came across another old man man who I'd never seen before, a nice man but with long hands, so to punish him a bit, I convinced him to take a bottle. After we found an agreement and in exchange for 100,000 L. I made him come. He Came immediately. I went to wash my hands in the bathroom. When I left the bathroom I came across Max I He took my hand and put it on him. All in a moment ... He was very excited. He told me: "See the effect you have on me? "" Yup, you have the same effect on me too! "... We immediately went back to work. I did some other table, nothing special. Then, surprise! Rico came to pick me up. We left with both cars. We couldn't just leave it to Marco, I didn't know if Remo wanted me to lend it. I followed Rico and we went to the same place in the woods. After I parked I got into his car. "I missed you, why did not you come yesterday?" "I worked, sometimes I have to work, you know! I cannot sleep anymore! Every night I'm off I spend it with you since we went out the first time. I do put shifts so that we can be together. " We spent the few hours caressing each other. We kissed very much and we also told many anecdotes that had happened in our lives. When he spoke to me I was enchanted, all facts related to his life before his marriage. I was enchanted in his presence, I actually don't remember almost anything except that at some point he asked me: "Do you still want me?" And I replied: "Of course! I missed you so much! "So we made love. It's great to make love to Rico! With him I really feel at ease. In bed, so to speak, that is, in the car, we have an extraordinary harmony: he always does what I really enjoy and he is so natural doing it, he doesn't have to make an effort to please me, we're perfectly compatible! I would never want to deprive myself of someone so special, I hope I never have to remove him from my life. Unfortunately, as usual when I'm with him, time flies at the speed of light and it's already dawn. I love the sunrise, but I hate it when arrives so suddenly while we are hugging. It really makes us suffer having to part from each other. *To us, the term "suffering" would be a bit exaggerated for the situation! But she's such a passionate woman!* It seemed like pulling away a magnet from a refrigerator. We are stuck to one another as if we were glued, it is as if we were bound by a kind of magnetic field, and when we have to part, it's really hard and tiring. I asked him if he could do me the favor to take me to my bank. But first, I had to ring my mother to get the right bank account coordinates of her account. Even though Rico was very late for him because he had to go back to work, he first drove me to have breakfast, then around 8:30 I called my mother and went to the bank where I made my deposit. Two million three hundred and fifty thousand liras I had earned. I had some pocket money for myself anyway and I really didn't need any cash ... Unfortunately, after being to the bank we had to leave and so I went home.

August 16, Thursday

When we said goodbye he sadly told me that during that week he would perhaps be a bit busy and it might be difficult to see me. " I'll try to come by as soon as I can " and then he said something that made me smile: "Try not to go out with other men in fact, just don't go out with other men! I'm jealous!" I really don't remember exactly how I answered but it was something like: okay okay, don't worry about a thing or something like that. I don't know if I can keep my promise, I think it will be very, very difficult. Let's hope that his commitments keep him busy to the point that he won't not notice if I do go out with someone else. When I arrived at Marco's they were all worried. They asked me where I had been. By now it was past nine o'clock and I always come back at about 6:30 or 7 in the morning when I went out with Rico. I explained that I had him take me to the bank to send money to my mother so she could pay some overdue installments. They knew that my family was a bit in economic difficulty, so fortunately that was it. Around lunch time I woke up to the delicious smell coming from the kitchen. Laura had cooked meatloaf which I adore. So I woke up in a hurry I washed up quickly and I was immediately in the front row to eat a small piece of that delicious meat loaf. After lunch Tiziana did the washing up and I helped her to wipe them dry and put them back in place. Then, given the nice day, we decided to take a walk with little Luca nearby home as the roads, being filled with trees, provided a really cool shade; back in the house, not having any air conditioning but only two small fans, it was very hot. I had a long chat with Tiziana about Rico and my feeling of complete well-being when I'm with him. So she finally opened up little and told me how he felt the same feeling with that guy I saw her with the last time. Of course, the most she had done was kissing him, but when it happened it felt exactly the feeling that I felt with Rico. I think the difference between us was that Tiziana felt well in her family, tightly rooted in it and therefore she didn't feel that sense of emptiness that I had instead. So I was at the mercy of her family's attention an that of both Rico and Remo. As if were totally empty inside. The afternoon was endless. Too much thinking! I tried to relax a bit but there was no way I could read a book or watch tv. Finally the evening arrived and I got ready for the nightclub. Marco and I drove there in Remo's car. Max was already there elegant and smelling real good as usual! He noticed I was a bit dazed and asked me if everything was fine. "Yea, I'm ok – I answered - now that I see you, I feel great!". Today the mechanic who had proposed me a free car-wash is back to see me. I devoted him some of my attentions. While I was talking to him, I asked him if he could try and fix my car that unfortunately had broken down. I really didn't know what was wrong with it. It made a strange noise, and at times it just stopped but I was pretty sure that I could manage to take it up to his workshop. Obviously Remos' car was in perfect condition, I was talking about Marco's. So we spent a lot of tables negotiating this exchange ... I think six or maybe seven. We see that the story of the damage of the car, the mechanic thought it wouldn't be much of a job and so we opted for a little job with my mouth. I wanted to trust him, he seemed like a good man. I satisfied him immediately. He was very satisfied with my work. He told me he would be waiting for me the next day in the morning. He left me his business card. Shortly after he went away with the excuse that he had to get up early. Later I saw the guy of the pools who pretended not to know me, maybe because I caught him with another girl! After all, he wasn't obliged to have tables with me only, but I actually was a little disappointed. Max came to my rescue: "Don't worry about the men who come here; for the most part they don't understand anything about women!! And then he whispered to my ear and: "You're just a fantastic woman!" My morale suddenly climbed way up there with the stars! Max, not only is really charming ... he is also really nice. Some girls instead find him a bit intrusive. Maybe they're angry with him because they have to give him a percentage of what they earn. He shares it with

Marco. That's why Max was so angry when Marco is not the club. It annoys him to have to share the money that Marco hasn't earned. During the night I had a few more tables, but nothing really special! Since some men who had won at the races tonight arrived we had a full night. I almost wasn't used to it anymore, as Rico had often come to get me before closing time. These gamblers sat wit a few girls including me. Luckily they wanted to sit in the sofas in front of the dance floor. They ordered some bottles to celebrate their win. They were all quite nice. They weren't even trying to touch us. They behaved well enough. One of them quietly asked me if he could invite me to go out with him. I answered that yes, he could take me out to dinner, but he had to talk to Max about it and after dinner he was to take me back to the club. "And if after dinner I took you in a hotel?" He asked me "Talk to Max about the club, then at dinner we can discuss all in details. You'll see that if we find an agreement agree, you'll be fully satisfied at the hotel!". We arrived at closing time with these. Finally! It was past five! I saw, as I went into the dressing room to get my things, that Alexander, the man who was with me, was talking to Max and Marco. Marco and I went home directly. This morning Max and the bouncer took the girl back to where they sleep. While I was heading back home with Marco, I asked him if Alexander had spoken to him about taking me out to dinner. He told me that the gentleman had spoken with Max and that he looked like a decent guy but that when arrived at the counter they had already finished speaking. So he said that I should ask Max directly. After all, if that guy had really wanted to take me out to dinner the next day, Max would have already told me. I told Marco that I would take the car to get fixed in the morning if he wanted. Marco was amazed. He wasn't expecting it. He said it was better to go with two cars. So he could see where this was mechanic was. He could drive Remo's. I could ride her so it would seem as if Marco's car was actually mine. Not only that, I could avoid having to do anything extra with the excuse that Marco was there to give me a ride back home. Although I was convinced that Marco was right, I was wondering about the real reason he was helping me: was he checking on me or was he really wondering whether or not to trust the mechanic? When we got home, I immediately went to sleep.

I am no longer used to working until 5:30. How exhausting! *Just like breaking rocks!*

August 17, Friday

By mid-morning I went with Marco to my client mechanic. We did as we had planned and I had him believe that Marco's car was mine. Marco got out of the car told the mechanic what he thought might be wrong with the car. I then told him that Marco would give me a ride to an appointment I had elsewhere. He told me to call him in the afternoon to find out when the car would be ready. I wonder whether he was disappointed by me not going there alone. Marco had me take him home and then I drove over to see Remo. He was always so busy. He was going back and forth for some late-comer customers of the resort carrying their sunbed or their lounge chair. He bought me an ice cream. However, since I could see that he was kind of busy, I then decided to go home. The little family, thinking that I would be with Remo had already had lunch. Laura immediately asked me if I'd had a fight with Remo. She immediately offered to get me something to eat on the fly, I thanked her so much, but having already had ice cream my stomach was quite full. Everyone was out shopping so, being left alone, I decided to have a nice, relaxing bath. I was in the water for at least an hour. A short while after I had dried off and got dressed, they all came back. I, Tiziana and her brother Luca went for a walk near the house. Tiziana thanked me so much for bringing her father's car to get fixed. Back home I called the mechanic. The car was almost ready. I could pick her up after 6. I decided to have dinner with Remo at the resort after picking up the car. At about 6:20 I went back to the mechanic with Marco and there were no problems: he explained all the work he had done to Marco. I thanked him and invited him to come see me at the nightclub. After leaving his store we exchanged cars and I drove Remo's car to the beach resort. As usual place there was no parking available so I followed a string of cars hat were lined up, but unfortunately the car got stuck right in the middle of some sand. *What a fool! A real fox!* In that spot the sand was too deep. Damn! Maybe it's because today is Friday the 17th?

I went to tell Remo who immediately came to see the damage I had caused. He tried to pull it out of the quagmire with a wooden pole but he didn't succed. He got a bit angry and called ACI. Who knows how much it's going to cost him. Damn, I blame the day, Friday 17 for all that happened, Remo instead blames me. Maybe he's at least 90% right. He was nervous throughout dinner; as his usual he cooked two burgers with a little salad. As I always did I split my dinner with Perlina the dog. Just to spend some time I got some small change and started playing the slot machines. Well, it was everything but an unlucky day because I won a myriad of small coins that added up to one hundred and fifty thousand liras. With a big smile on my face I told Remo he could keep them to pay for the tow truck, but Remo, a real gentleman changed the money with bank notes and said, "Don't worry, I'll take care of it. With this money you've won, buy something for yourself!". And so, I was happy once again. I went to work wearing a big smile. Max was already there and so were Marco and the bouncer. Many girls had gone out to dinner with that group of horse race gamblers. I asked Max if Alexander, the gentleman whom I'd had the table with was among them I, but he was vague about it, as if he didn't know who was at the dinner. I wonder if he did it on purpose! Was Max getting jealous of me or did Alexander not have a good time with me? If he had come back to the club, I would have tried to find out. Apart from winning at the slot machines the evening began badly. I was back a in the dumps. I had a couple of tables with a young boy, he had just turned 18 recently and rather shy: we had a chat and then he wanted to have a slow dance with me. I could tell he didn't have a lot of money and after the second table he left ... too bad he was nice and cute. After that, the old man of the bottle came back; who knows, maybe he hadn't given up yet and still wanted to get some pleasure with me. After a couple of tables I proposed to give him a massage in exchange for a bottle. He agreed on condition that I would even let him touch me but I agreed only to let him touch my breasts. After the massage I immediately went to wash my hands. Max made the time of the bottle end earlier than it was supposed to. Was he jealous? So I spent some time with a girl who had been sitting in the sofas. Surprisingly, the pool salesman asked of me again. When we went to sit, I asked him if he had been okay with me the last time and why he'd had a table with another girl the night before. "Com'on, don't be jealous now! - He said - I had met that girl before you. I'm a guy who's got many friends, take it or leave it!". "Yea, yea, I said, I'll take take it, it was just a joke!". So we chatted for only three tables. But neither he nor I were very comfortable there. Then, I did some other tables. Fortunately, this evening was getting to an end. Marco left early once again saying he wasn't feeling well, so Max would take me back home. Just think if Rico comes just when Max is taking me me home, but unfortunately tonight Rico didn't come by. I miss him! Finally I had three tables with a postal worker. At first he was shy and didn't say a word, then he gained confidence and became an octopus, and I put him back on the right path, explaining him that he should pay separately for all the extras. Who knows maybe I was too direct and abrupt! ... *Really?! An elephant in a china shop! Diplomacy is not your cup of tea!* ... At about five fifteen, all the girls who were in the club had left with the bouncer. Many had their evening paid and would not come back. As it had already happened to us Max and I were alone once again. I asked if he was jealous of me. As an answer, he approached me and started kissing me. I got excited as usual. He undressed me and we made love on the sofa. We both came together. Then he said, "With you it's beautiful! You get me so excited but maybe I've already told you. Wait here, I'll go to the bathroom for a moment, I still want you, but I have to change my protection. Want to come once again with me? Don't cool down baby!". As soon as I heard these words, I got excited once again to the idea of him inside of me once more, he was really back in a flash and he was super excited. This time he took me from behind, touching my breasts with one hand and stroking me with the other in the front. Generally I don't like this position, but he is so sensual, and he even managed to make me come. We were really satisfied. I put my clothes back on and he took me to breakfast.

August 18, Saturday

Max drove me home. I immediately went to sleep waking up at lunchtime. Marco gave me the third degree, perhaps he realized that I had come back home late, or who knows. The fact is that he wanted to know if I had been with Max. "We only had a chat and then he treated me to breakfast at the bar. That's why I came back late, "I said innocently,"But why are you asking me all these questions?" So Marco told me that some girls went to the owner to complain, saying that Max would almost force them to have sex with him, and in return he would guarantee them a steady flow of work and wouldn't be laid off; he would give them more work and protection. I absolutely couldn't believe it. Max is so fascinating that I really doubt he needs to 'force' women to have sex with him. He inspires sex from all his pores ... well! After lunch they all had a nap. Then, in the late afternoon we all went to the sea ... Remo had reserved seats for us. So while Tiziana and Marco cleaned the place up, we had a good time at the beach; the little one behaved like a real good boy in the stroller under the shade of the beach umbrella, Tiziana and I sitting in the lounge chairs next to Luca, watching him, and the other brother made a dive after another in the sea. Lucky him, what energy! I just couldn't do it, I have low blood pressure! ... *Yea, whenever you decide to!* ... When they went home I was left alone with Remo, and I did not want to go through another third degree again. I had a shower and then I had dinner there with Remo and we talked about the quarrels between the bartenders: Max angry with Marco who was always sick, convinced he was pretending, and Marco trying to discredit him in the eyes of the owner making up stories between the girls and him. And they both tried to put me in the middle of all this while instead, I tried to stay out of it. I went to work at the usual time and Max was furious. Marco wouldn't come. "At least his wife cleans up the place!" I pretended not to hear the sentence. "If you want, I can give you a hand at the tables. When they are not with customers" "Let's see if I need to, I won't distract you from your work. Thanks anyway." Also the owner of the club came over to help Max out. Luckily, I worked most of the evening. At one point I had a table with an elderly man who spoke to me for five, maybe six tables. He wanted to know me better: he asked me if I played sports, if I knew any foreign languages, if I had traveled, what studies I did, he asked me a bit of everything. I answered all his questions, so in the meantime time was going by and I was doing more and more tables just because this guy didn't actually know who I was and where I lived. But then, my life was not that interesting or particularly unique. He told me about his work: recruiting new people to enlarge the existing intelligence workforce. To support his thesis, he had me believe that in Rome near the university there was a place that everyone could see, a small door, giving access to the largest station of the Italian intelligence ... *How sweet, you really believe anyone and everything that comes out of their mouth! A little helpless puppy. Wake up!* ... And he also asked me that if I could be interested in that kind of career, to meet up the morning after so to have the first interview with him. Later if I passed more tests, I would attended special courses and I would be hired for a mission. I accepted. He convinced me. It had always been one of my dreams: to become an undercover secret agent. I was very excited and curious. Then George the bar owner came by. "I want you to know me better!" He said. So we did a few tables together, I drank many juices, as my usual. He told me something about his life, his qualities, that he was a good guy, a good worker ... he was in some way hansome too. The only defect he had was that he was a little chubby and I really cannot stand fat people. I must have some problems with weight and food. Maybe because I've always seen my mother overeating since childhood. She did it because she was nervous because of her misunderstandings with my father, I think. He couldn't stand the fact that my mother was fat. And so I'm always afraid of getting fat myself. Only here I manage to feel a little more comfortable, away from the problems of my house living with a second family, with plenty of admirors and with my pockets full. I promised the guy to visit with him at his bar. Only a short short visit ... no harm, I thought. When he left I had other tables with different men, short tables, maybe two drinks or so. They were all somewhat annoyed, bitter and disappointed. Who knows what they thought I could actually do for them. It's not like I could change their life in twenty or forty minutes, maybe I could manage to give them a good time for a while ... yes sometimes the guys who come here trust you, they want to let off steam and find someone who understands them. I listen and try to comfort them, and differntly to what my colleagues do, I never tease them. Theother girls are clever: they tell them what they want to hear, like "You're a great guy, someone special, I get a real feeling for you!" And then maybe "I have my grandmother, my brother, a sick aunt or big debts at home. Or: I need to send money to help my very large family. Could you help me out? Only a loan, I wouldn't be asking if I really didn't need to!" Cheating, I really hate that. I am more the nurse kind of type, friendly voice, funny, positive thinking, masseuse: a mutual exchange. Some girls instead stick to a man and drive him broke. Then they change nightclub and start allover again. They are heartless, don't they have any conscience? Let's forget it ... The night was over, since the owner of the club was also there, Max and I took the girls home. Then Max asked me if I wanted to go with him to a meeting; why not! We drove to a parking lot of a supermarket and there he took out a briefcase; he then showed me there were watches inside. "You know ... just to make some extra cash I have a friend who travels a lot and brings me things to sell. These are identical to original Rolex watches and in this bag there are synthetic diamonds. Wait here, I have a delivery to make! I will not be long, only five minutes. Ok? "By then I was saying. "Yes, yes, I'll rest a bit!" After about 10 minutes he came back. He told me that everything had gone well and that another jeweler friend of his had taken the whole lot. He was amazed that I wasn't interested at all in his dealings. For me, everyone does they want and must accept the consequences of their actions. "Yup!" I said, "You're really a special woman ... if only I weren't married ..." I dropped the subject. Yes for some good sex he was perfect, but for something more, I really didn't know him well enough, and he didn't seem quite appropriate ... too many women in his life for my taste.

August 19, Sunday

At home I slept a little ... I set the alarm clock and I woke up with difficulty, I took a shower and I got ready. I didn't say anything about my date with the secret agent to my little family. I had a short walk and then I went to my appointment. Shortly after, my date arrived. He told me that his car had broken down and he asked me if I had one. I told him to wait for me and I went to Remo. The beach resort wasn't too far away. I asked him if I could borrow his car for a while. He had it pulled out of the sand the day before. I promised him I would be extremely careful and that I'd really look after it. He lent it to me. I'm excellent at asking for things. I can be very persuasive ... I then picked up Ernesto of the secret services, *Yea ... sure!* He asked me if the car was mine. I explained him that I had borrowed it. He complimented me on overcoming obstacles in such a quick and easy way, showing me how deep down inside of me, I had what it takes to be an agent who copes with difficult situations he might run into. He invited me to lunch, we left Bellaria: the restaurant was a bit isolated but there were many cars in the parking lot so I felt safe enough. We ate quite well but when we asked for the bill, he asked me if I could lend him forty thousand liras. Luckily I had fifty thousand with me. So, since I really didn't feel like looking cheap with the restaurateur nor with this character, I lent him the money. Who knows, I thought, maybe it's a test! *Yea, you can count on it!* He invited me over to his house. There, we would talk away from prying eyes and ears ... I almost believed him. We parked in front of his house and we went inside, it was a small villa divided in different apartments. He didn't pull up the blinds, he turned on the lights and then he got two silver goblets from the cupboard in the living room. He poured me a cold Martini that tasted strangely sweet. I had never tasted it before … and, I don't know how it could happen, but we ended up on his bed. I have vague memories of what happened. A feeling like a slobbering old man who behaved like an octopus. Who knows what he wanted to do, but his penis no longer worked the way it should have. Fortunately, he gave up right away. He justified himself by telling me that it was all part of the test. We got dressed after a short while later somebody knokcked at the door. Who could it be? It was his daughter who was furious with her father. She made it quite clear that he was used to paying for women and she called me a whore. I was shocked! He glanced at me hinting that I should go along with what was happening. While she went to the kitchen to wash the glasses, he said that I had behaved very well and that he had a first small mission for me. He would come back to the club to give me instructions and detailed times. He showed me to the door. I then drove back to Marco's. I was furious especially with myself. How could I have let someone fool me like that. *I wonder how … since you never believe what your customers tell you!* But I was torn between believing him, and not, thinking then that I hadn't been fooled, and that perhaps this was actually all a cover for him. One more night at the club and then I would spend a quiet day with Remo. I was really looking forward to it! These days I'm a bit stressed out. At Marco's home I pretended everything is fine with me, Tiziana spoke to me about his friend Dario, confessing to be in love with him: they sometimes kissed. At the moment, she is not free to leave whenever she wants because she has to look after her little brother Dario, so she really hopes he's going to wait for her. They haven't made big promises to each other and, so far it seems that he has never ever asked for more. She asked about me, I told her that I was a bit sad because I hadn't seen Rico in a while … perhaps he had to work. After all, tomorrow I would be with Remo as I do every Monday … I'd rather Rico had come back after Tuesday. Oh yes, Tiziana was right. That evening I wanted to give the car back to Remo. He told me that I could keep it because he really didn't need it. But since the next day was Monday and he usually came to pick me up I thought it would be better if he had his car back. We had dinner together. As usual I split my two hamburgers with Perlina. It's a sweet little dog and it's always glad to see me. Marco and Max were already at the club. The bouncer had gone to pick up the girls. The night began in a quiet way. I, as usual, did a few insignificant tables. Then, a decent looking guy who went straight to the point came over to me and asked me what I could do for him. "I'm not a whore, but maybe you're a cop!" I replied. You know ... *you're really weird! Are you surprised he made a point-blank question just like that?! I know that sometimes your head is somewhere in the clouds ... it forgets the kind of work you do!* He changed his tone but he resumed his strange negotiations with me. I didn't give in! So he stood up and immediately changed table! While I was going to the bathroom, I called Max. When he joined me I told him about what had just happened and he replied that I'd made the right choice because lately undercover cops have been hanging around to keep an eye on what's going on in nightclubs premises. I always had to keep in mind that the rule was that nothing can go on inside the club, just innocent talking with the customers. Then, George, that chubby guy came by. His bar was really nice though. I had to earn back some money and he certainly wasn't a policeman. I took the initiative to kiss him, he had really soft lips soft ... maybe we had already kissed, I don't remember. Max came to take the order right while we were kissing; he touched my arm and my heart started racing. We were quietly talking until he brought the drinks. Then, on my own initiative I unbuttoned his pants and started touching him. He didn't pull back and as we kissed he came. I went to the bathroom to wash up. Then when I came back he told me that it had been wonderful, that he liked me very much he always thought about me. I took the opportunity to ask him if he could lend me 100,000 lire. Since he had to pay for the drinks, he could only give me half of it, and he could give me the rest when I go to see him at his bar. I definetely agreed, but not on Monday. At least, I thought to myself, I have recovered the money that Ernesto, the fake 007 had extorted from by deception. We did three other tables. We chatted, danced and we kissed some more. What can I do, I do like his lips and his way of kissing. Then he left ... he had to work early the day after; he opened up the bar ... too bad ... I was at ease and relaxed with him, if he had stayed, the evening would have gone by in a flash. As Max escorted me to my tables, he would touch me and I would always get excited ... I wonder if he did it because he was attraced to me or because that way I could be in a better mood with my new customers ... I had a soft spot for him. At the end of the night, since the bouncer had taken home the girls who were left in the club and Marco had called in sick once again, Max and I were alone once again. We immediately stuck to one another like glue, as two people who never do it. *It seems as if you are transforming it into a new art form!* We both had great desire. First he possessed me as I like it, in the classical position and between one kiss and one we came. Then he turned me over, took his own protection off and took me from behind. "I don't know if I like it from behind!" I told him. But by touching me in the font with one hand and touching my breast with his other, he made me relax so much to make me come in that strange and uncomfortable position, almost never practiced, while he filled my neck with kisses. It's always great to have him inside of me! Yes perhaps even behind! We went to breakfast and then he took me home. "Don't get too tired with Remo, tomorrow!" He said. "Yes, don't worry, after all we've done I think I'll take a rest tomorrowt!" I replied. But actually, I really knew I wouldn't!

August 20, Monday

I woke up late, I was exhausted, too much sex, I wasn't used to it. *Maybe not before, but now ...* I called Remo. "Finally, he said, I thought you had forgotten about us" ... He starts ... *Actually he is the only one who would be entitled to!* I said something very nice and immediately ran into the bathroom to get ready. All washed up and smelling good, I wore a very nice dress Tiziana had lent me. I hope that by being with Remo today I'll manage not to think about Rico. He was sweet as usual, he took me to a really fancy restaurant. "What are we celebrating today?" I asked, all he pulled out a box ... inside there was a small ring with a small diamond ... I think! Yes, I could tell it was real after he showed me the guarantee. "I hope we will stay together, he said, or perhaps you are thinking of leaving me when you come back to Rome?" "No way, you fool!" I replied. "How could I leave you, I'm really good with you !!" ... *and with your gifts ...* so after lunch we took a walk that took us right in front of our usual hotel. We went up in our room and we spent the afternoon making love. Whenever I tried to move away from him, Remo grabbed me and started kissing once again, touching me and making love to me. What a great afternoon! We even took a shower together, he literally washed me. "You're my little doll, he said, I always want to wash and comb you and do everything to you! I want to stay with you forever. You know I always think about you when I'm at work. Are you behaving at the nightclub? "" Of course, you know I just want you! "I replied. Luckily, he bought it. After this afternoon of fire we went out to dinner. This ring is beautiful! I didn't do anything but watch it shine all evening long. I was in seventh heaven! We were both tired and, after dinner, we went back to the hotel. Although we were really exausted, we made love one more time before falling asleep. We slept embraced.

August 21, Tuesday

At six thirty, as usual, the alarm went off. Remo got up, took a shower and got ready to go to work at the resort, I fell asleep again. Upon awakening I found an inviting breakfast resting on a small table. There was everything I could think of: croissants, coffee and milk, orange juice and fruit. There was also a note that said to get up slowly and that I could comfortably stay in the room as long as I wanted to. He had already paid for everything as always. He had also sent me lots of kisses and left me the car keys, that way I could be freer. Maybe he left them because he knew that Marco often missed work and he was afraid that someone else would take me home, and who knows, maybe would take advantage of the situation. *Come on, how can you think of such?*

Every once in a while you connect to reality! So I had breakfast. I stayed a while longer in that comfortable bed where our scents got mixed together. I watched television for some time, I took a shower and came back home with his car. Here, I immediately told Tiziana about the ring: "I will be a good girl I told him, just work from now on!" By now, it was lunch time, but I was not hungry after my big breakfast. I don't know exactly what I did that afternoon, I think I fantasized about my future with Remo. I stayed home while my new family had gone to do some errands. When I came back I chatted some more with Tiziana. She, like a good sister, was very happy for me. In the evening Tiziana helped me to get ready for work as usual: she said I was much more beautiful than usual. I was different, I looked beaming! Tonight I went to the club with Marco who seems to feel better. I thought I would leave the ring at home as it might get in the way ... it would be safer there anyway. Max was smelling so good and he was as charming as ever. He noticed too that I was really beaming that night. So, perhaps being even more attracted to me, he introduced me to new customers in ways that sounded better and better. As usual we played our personal touch game us whenever it was possible. I always got so excited to see him and even smell his perfume and it was enough for him to touch me, even only on my hand, to arouse me more and more.

Strangely enough, I had only quiet tables today. It's not that the club was overflowing with customers indeed, but Max hijacked the majority of customers to me. Just as well, I worked, spending time and playing with Max. I really liked my job! *Job so to speak!* At three o'clock, with my huge surprise, Rico came to pick me up. Suddenly all my good intentions towards Remo vanished into thin air although I realized I was a bit angry with him. I followed him anyway. In the car I asked him if anything had happened to him, "Did you forget about me?" "Do you come here to pick me up and play with me whenever you find some spare time and you don't know what to do?" He jammed on the brakes. I almost slammed my head on the dashboard. Luckily he wasn't going that fast. He immediately took my head in his hands and, looking into my eyes told me: "I could never do that to you! You must believe me when I tell you that you are special to me! I never cheated on my wife before! For you I really lost my head! "And gave me a very intense kiss. We went in the woods, to our usual spot, I thought about what he had said, and he seemed sincere. We immediately started off just where we had left ... as always feeling completely at ease. We kissed for a long time, until we just couldn't resist any longer and we made love. It was great as usual. I came, and I felt completely satisfied like I always do when I'm with him. He also came ... out of me as usual. We were very affectionate to one another until sunrise. Unfortunately, it was time to part and this always arrives too soon. He took me to breakfast insisting I really should eat something. I made him happy and so I did. I was a bit sad because we had to part. I don't know how it happened, before I got out of Rico's car in front of Marco's house I told him: "Will we ever spend more time together?" "I really want to spend more time with you too, I want to know everything about you. It'll happen soon, you'll see. I promise!" Then, I went home.

August 22, Wednesday

They were all sleeping ... I felt a bit confused. I was on a terrible guilt trip. I just couldn't get to sleep. Finally, after an endless wait, my little sister Tiziana woke up, I immediately told her about what had happened the night before. She had already figured it out as her dad had come back home alone without me. " I just couldn't keep my promise Tiziana ... What do you think, shall I give him back the ring?" She immediately answered me with her forthcoming and neutral style: "No! Are you're crazy, wait!" And so she spent all morning trying to convince me to take my time. Basically, Rico was already married. He would probably, indeed certainly, never leave his wife and children. Then, on my return to Rome, the distance would eventually separate us. Suddenly, looking at the calendar, I realized that my cycle was late. Typically, my cycle was always on the same day. But this time it was already ten days late. I practically panicked. As they were all home, I waited after lunch to go out for a walk with Tiziana. As soon as we went out with the little one in the stroller along the tree-lined streets near her house, I immediately confessed my fears to her. Today is worry-day for me! *Maybe you're the one who's looking for trouble...!* Just like a good and wise sister would do, she advised me to talk to Remo about it. When we were back home, I drove over to the resort. I told him I needed to talk to him in private so we went for a walk on the waterfront. I told him I was late and he was amazed. He couldn't explain how it was possible since he had always come out. However, there could always be a possibility. He shocked me! He immediately took the situation in his hands and told me: "If you actualy are pregnant, stop working immediately and wait for me in Rome. When I finish my job here at the resort, I'll come and marry you! I love you, don't worry!" What he told me, reassured me indeed. I am very lucky to have such a gentle, generous, helpful and understanding man near me. I'd better not chase him away by doing something stupid. I spent the whole afternoon under the beach umbrella and Remo sometimes came by with ice cream or something to drink. He pampered me a whole lot. He was so sweet to me! From the moment I told him about the possible pregnancy he immediately became much more considerate! That evening he insisted that I ate both the two burgers and even a small piece of bread and a little salad. I ate everything, I did not want to contradict him. It was time to go to work for me. I got ready and went to the club. I really didn't feel at ease. My belly was big ...I was too full. I felt bloated! Today, unlike other days I wasn't looking for Max's touch. But he behaved as he usually did so I didn't tell him about my delay so that he wouldn't get suspicious ... it wasn't any of his business anyway. When he tried to touch me I tried to behave as usual and I touched him back. I wonder if he realized that tonight I never made the first move. If he had asked me about it I'd have made up an excuse. But he seemed not to have noticed that something was wrong. I did a few tables but, feeling strange, I always preferred to sit on benches in front of the dance floor. When my clients wanted to take me in the darker and more private parts of thje club, I gently explained them I wasn't feeling well and that if they had come back another night, I would have made them happy. Who knows, maybe this was my last night there. Luckily, I stayed right there in the front, and around midnight Remo came out of nowhere. He almost gave me a heart attack. I new something strange would happen. We did a couple of tables together. He had come to tell me that if I had any kind of problem or simply I felt tired he would immediately take me home at Marco's. Without getting into details, I had already told him I wasn't feeling that well. And that if there was need he should accompany me back home. All this wasn't for free, but it was paid handsomely by Remo himself. He had been very pleased to see me sitting in the sofas in sight. "Well, I told you that I was behaving well at work, didn't you believe me?" "Of course, darling, I just came to see if you were all right, if you needed something. I have already spoken with Marco: If you're not up to even standing up, he should immediately take you home, and I recommend you not to get to tired too!" After a tender kiss he left. The next morning he had to get up early. It was an evening full of surprises. At three o'clock Rico came by. I wasn't expecting him. I was really happy, especially about the fact that he was taking me away from the club. On arriving at the pine forest, I told him I was late. He was surprised and scared, "Aren't you on the pill?" He asked. "No! But you always came out ... or at least most of the times, right? "I said ironically. At first he did not know what to do, he says. It was very awkward and funny as well. A policeman who had subordinates, used to giving orders and keeping everything under control had behaved so carelessly. How could it be it possible, he wondered. I quickly reassured him by telling him that I would raise my child with my boyfriend. He would also marry me! "At least we will be almost equal!" I said a little angry. Who knows why I said that. All in all, I was officially with Remo, what would I care about Rico? Maybe it was just sex with him, as with Max. I got a slap in my face and Immediately started crying. The slap wasn't that hard, and he was amazed by his reaction to my provocation as well. "I had never touched a woman with a finger! You really make me lose my mind. I know what you said is the truth! I'm sorry! I didn't want to do it! It's not my fault if I have a past still in the present. When I first met you I tried to resist. And to tell myself that I am a rock. I really don't know what happened to me, but I just lost my head with you! I feel something really deep for you. Did I hurt you?" "No! "I answered him so I wouldn't give him any satisfaction, while the tears kept on coming down. "I know you don't believe me when I tell you these things, but that's the truth. I will try to prove it to you as soon as I can! I don't even know myself what I'll do! I don't want to lose you, and if I had a child I wouldn't want to lose him either because he would be the result of the strong feelings I feel for you ... that really confuses me. I wish you could feel what I feel for you!" At this point he started kissing me and caressing my face. He kissed me all over my eyes and cheeks. All tender kisses. I stopped crying. "I won't make you cry anymore for life! I want to see you happy! "So he kept on kissing me everywhere and started taking my clothes off. He caressed my belly and then spread my legs. I felt embarassed but his sweetness made me won me over. He began to lick me until I came. He said I had a very good flavor. I told him it wasn't right that I had came alone and that I didn't know what his flavor was. So he moved on top of me. And, after making sure I was comfortable and I really wanted his semen in my mouth he went back licking me. I did the same. This time, we both came. He immediately asked me "What flavor do I have? Is it good?" " Yes, you have a good taste of sea water! "The rest of the night passed him to fill me with kisses and caresses. I felt loved! Completely loved!

August 23, Thursday

Unfortunately we got dressed at dawn and he took me back to Marco's. When I got out of the car we said nothing but goodbye. We didn't know what to say, as if we had got lost. I cannot explain, a strange feeling, like never before. At home I immediately went to sleep. When everyone woke up, I went to buy a pregnancy test with Tiziana. I took a package of two. I did the: The first one was negative. The second was the same. Why I had neither children nor menstruation? I couldn't get it. I asked

Tiziana to do me a big favor by, to take me to her gynecologist. In the afternoon, without telling our secrets to her parents with little Luca in the stroller we went to her gynecologist who was a woman. After a thorough examination and a few questions she explained me that the delay could have resulted from the sudden weight loss. I shouldn't worry because my menstruation would be back real soon. She was very kind and she really took a big burden off my back. And she did not even want to be paid for the visit, saying she couldn't take any money from a guest of Tiziana's family. I liked Bellaria and its inhabitants more and more ... I wonder how it would be to live there! In the evening I had come a bit of a stomach ache and a short while later, here's my cycle. Damn! if I had waited just one more day all this mess wouldn't have happened. Tiziana advised me now to go and speak with Remo and so I did. I drove to Remo's and told him the news and he answered me: "From now on, however, we will always use a condom! It's generally best to have children when you're married!" I felt a little bad about what he said but, in the end he was right. This evening instead of dinner I had a huge ice cream, just to feel a little better. At the usual time, I went to work. This evening Marco and Max are both there. Max, after some time, while nobody was looking, softly asked me if there was something wrong with me. He said he asked me because, since a few nights before he saw something strange in me. "Did I do anything that made you angry?" I simply said that I was nervous because I had my things. I did only few tables. Max, maybe because I had told him I wasn't feeling well, wasn't unbridledly publicizing me among customers as he usually did. Who knows, maybe deep down he cared for me! At the end of the night I only had a limited number of tables, say just enough to not get fired. I came back home with Marco. I didn't want to drive, and so I left the car near Remo's resort.

August 24, Friday

Today I spent the whole morning sleeping, when I woke up it was just before one o'clock. I asked Tiziana if she had any painkillers. She only had a couple of pills left. She gave them to me. I told her I would buy some that evening and I would give them back to her, but she told me I didn't need to. I had to buy them anyway. I also needed to buy some pads that had almost run out. In the afternoon we went to the pharmacy together always with Luca in the stroller. Since I hadn't had anything to eat since the night before, I was quite hungry at dinner and so I exceptionally ate a forkful of pasta as I always do when I felt like eating. In the evening, as usual, we went to the club with Marco and having taken a good deal lot of painkillers I somewhat felt better. I wanted to make up for the lost work so I urged Max to make me work more. He sent me several new customers. The guy of the railways also came back again: we did three or four tables with the promise that I would touch him for always for 100,000 lire and that's how it went. I quickly washed my hands. Then he started the usual spiel that seeing each other that way was not what he really wanted, that he would marry me if only I wanted him to. He was getting a bit too heavy as usual. But suddenly I had an idea: I told him that before we could get married we had to get engaged. And that if he wanted me to get engaged to him, he should offer me a bottle. *You're a genius, no doubt about it! I think that there must be something in that nightclub that makes people see all those donkeys fly!* So he immediately called Max and ordered a bottle. He tried to get me drunk by making a toast after another. What really happened was that all that alcohol got mixed with the painkillers I had taken, so at some point I felt really bad. Luckily I managed to run to the bathroom and throw up. I immediately felt better. When I came back to the table I told the guy what had just happened so he eased off on his enthusiasm a bit. Good! I could not bear him any longer. He kept on asking me for a date for the next day. I took advantage of the fact that I was feeling bad to tell him that it was better if he came by the club in the evening, perhaps to organize something for the next day. Just because I was not feeling well ... eventually he left.

I did a few more tables. They were all little octopusses t 'polyps, but nothing I couldn't handle. Customers asking who knows what and for free. Impossible! Fortunately, even this night was over.

August 25, Saturday

I came back home with Marco. I slept most of the morning, I'm not used to vomiting and when I do, I feel relly exhausted after. At lunch I didn't eat anything. After I sat on the bed chatting with Tiziana. I confessed to her that I was a bit puzzled because since Remo learned that there no longer was or there never was a child, he never showed up again. According to Tiziana perhaps he was just tto busy. At dinner I ate a bit of meatloaf. Then I went to the club with Marco. We took a longer ride than usual to pick up other girls. When we got to the nightclub Max was already there. I did it a couple of tables with the guy of the pools. He asked me to go out with him again. I told him that I had to think about it. So he got restless and left the table with me. What did he expect ... after he had mocked me. Did he want to do it again? *In that place, it's quite normal to have an ax to grind ... in real life too in most cases!* After that Then then I had other tables with normal customers. By mid-night, Max took me to a private couch where there was a man in his fifties waiting for me: a bit chubby, but very elegantly dressed. He bluntly asked me an immediate exchange: "I'll do what you want if you can make me come three times. For you now here I'll put a thousand liras, and you'll get another hundred and fifty if you succeed." I accepted saying that we needed privacy, so he should order a bottle. He immediately called Max and ordered the most expensive one. Indeed Max made two trips because the strange guy had ordered two. So we had eight tables time to be together without being interrupted or

75

disturbed. I started to unbutton his pants. He asked me if he could touch me. "Granted, but only out!" So I lowered my panties; I had an internal tampon: everything was dry! We began to touch each other. He was good at touching. With one hand touched my nipples passing from one to the other and with the other hand he toched me in the front. I liked it so much that I started kissing him. After a while we both came. He would not let me go to the bathroom, so I used the champagne to wash my hands down ... it was alcohol after all! He immediately put the hand he had touched me with in front of his mouth and said I tasted good. Then he pushed my head on his penus telling me to pull it up once again because he still had a great desire. Meanwhile he had begun to touch me better than before. What a maniac! I really enjoyed it though! *In fact they are the maniacs ... or maybe you are a nymphomaniac?* As soon as he was hard again, and I must say it didn't take much, I started to touch him, I preferred doing that rather than licking a stranger. So we came together once again. What a strong guy! As I had done before, I washed off with champagne whereas he again tasted the fingers that had touched me. Then he himself wanted to go to the bathroom. And if I wanted, I could go there too. But then, I didn't need to. While he was in the bathroom, Max came by wondering about what we were doing. And I said: "Nothing special." And he told me then telling me not to pass up this client because he really had a lot of money. Shortly after, the guy was back. We chatted a bit between drinks. He had a small industry that produced special lenses for various uses. And he exported worldwide. I told him a few things about me. Then we chatted a bit of everything, the club, Bellaria, Rome. At four-thirty he left telling me that he had a family lunch the next day. "Won't you ask me for the rest of the money?" He asked. "No, the deal was three times and you came only twice." Amazed by my straight answer, he said that sometimes he would take me out to dinner and then bring me back to the club. I accepted. I wish all customers were like that! I did some other tables then, luckily the lights went on and it was time to close the club. I came home with Marco.

August 26, Sunday

Upon arriving, I immediately went to sleep. I decided to take a walk in the morning with Tiziana that luckily, was always forthcoming. She had agreed to go and see the guy with the bar. I gave her his business card; she knew the city quite well so she took me there quite easily. Luca, being Sunday stayed at home with his parents. As we were waking I told Tiziana that Rico too had disappeared, yet he still believed that I was pregnant. "One more reason to stay with Remo" Tiziana said. When we arrived at Giorgio's bar he was really amazed, he really did'nt expect me to go there any more. He gave us a super welcome and, since it was just before lunch, he had us sit at his best table and brought us drinks with appetizers. We both chose non-alcoholic aperitifs. Because George was alone at the bar, he was forced to come back and forth between us and the counter. We stayed there for half an hour then we had to be back before lunch. I went up to greet him. I gave him a kiss on the cheek, saying that if he were free he could come and see me in the evening at the local. He agreed to go back there just because I went to see him, or else he said he would no longer come. He was really nice and he also gave me a packet with pastery telling me to take it to my host family. Then he also gave me an envelope and told me to open it in private. I was very curious! I put it in my purse … I would open it later on at home. When we got home, as usual, I didn't have the heart to have any food. I sat on my bed reading. My new little family in the afternoon would go and see their grandparents. They invited me to go along with them but , I told them I still had a stomach ache. So I stayed all afternoon alone. I didn't do anything special, I watched tv for a while, I felt extremely confused. Suddenly, both Remo and Rico were gone. So I decided to leave a note at home and walk to the resort. I arrived just before dinner. Remo seemed a little different. I gave him his car keys. Since I had not felt good I had always gone and come back from work with Marco. We agreed to see each other the next day directly at lunchtime. It seemed that Remo was a somewhat different. I told him I was not feeling well and that I didn't feel like having dinner. He didn't worry much about it. I had no need for his care ... I could get along just fine alone! How strange men are! I just don't understand them. *Relax, you're not the only one!* Sometime before the opening of the nightclub I decided to take a walk: I noticed that the place was already open. Or rather, a side door was unlocked. I got inside and, to my surprise I found Max over a Russian girl having sex on the sofas. I rushed out, I closed the outer door and get on with my walk. I showed up at the right time at the club, and Max looked a little embarrassed. "Did you see us together?" he asked "Yes", I answered "Luckily it was just me, I also closed the door. You took a big risk ... big you know they are doing investigations on you because they think you take all the girls to bed." So he asked me to quickly tell him about this story. I told him that I was asked several questions about what I knew about him and the girls and whether we had gone to bed together, I denied of course. And I also defended him because I did not believe it possible that he needed to force the girls to go to bed with him. Max thanked me in a without making too many ceremonies. I pretended I didn't really care and went back to my seat with the girls on the couch; by now, I thought Max was no longer interested in me! He was really enjoying himself! I, too, that night wanted to find someone just for fun. Who knows, maybe just out of spite! Shortly after the opening of the club Giorgio came to see me. Differently from what I usually do, I decided to take him to the hidden sofas. After ordering our drinks I started to kiss him and we toched each other a bit. He started to touch me first, he was very good, I was warming up so I started to touch him myself. At one point we stopped and I asked to take a bottle just so we could be safe for four drinks He strangely accepted so when Max came we asked for the bottle and when he brought it we asked him not to be disturbed. Who knows what Max thought, I had never made such a request until then. The fact is that Giorgio was a good boy and I felt some shame ... what if someone had suddenly popped up? After a toast we started kissing and touching, he was very good and I got excited and I was very good too ... he told me between a kiss and another. We came together. Wow, how cool! When business mixes with pleasure it's really exciting! I went to wash my hands as usual. When I came back he had gone into the bathroom to get himself together. He was pleasantly surprised by my initiative. He thought it was in some way linked to his envelope containing L. 100,000. I told him that I felt deeply offended. Actually I had forgotten to open the envelope. I opened the handbag I had brought with me, and in fact the envelope was still intact. He apologized over and over, and turned red like a lobster. To cut it short, I told him that his punishment would be to do some other tables with me. George told me that even though he was very happy to spend some more time with me, on the other hand maybe it wasn't such a good idea to give money to those loansharks. "We could spend it for ourselves," he said. I simply dropped the matter. I just wasn't interested. I just wanted time to go by. On Sunday I was always tired and was really looking forward to the night to end. After a few more tables, when Giorgio left, I chatted with other customers. Fortunately, I was on a bench in front of the dance floor when at about two Rico showed up. I was always lucky with him. He had never found me in the dark, hidden sofas, with other men. I had always got away with it. We left the room and his car went to the usual place in the woods. I just can't help it; it's like everything seems to go automatically into the background. Is it my heart that takes over? I didn't say anything. When we arrived he told me that he loved me and that he wanted our son. I tearfully told him it was just a long delay as the gynecologist said, perhaps due to the fact that I had lost too much weight. "So now you have your period?" He asked. "Yes" I replied. "Then I can you love freely tonight" "But isn't it groce?" "I want all of you, I like you completely, remember I've already told you: I think I love you!" So he started to kiss and undress me. To avoid staining the car before we went to make love in the water. Like the first time. Then he picked me up and took me to the car. Here he placed a towel, and he started to love me till dawn. I lost count of how many times we came. Strange to say, but he always maintained an erection. When we got dressed, he told me: "See I told you the truth, I want you just the way you are!" He took me to breakfast and then mmediately to Marco's. We both felt very relaxed.

August 27, Monday

Remo had just rang the intercom. Tiziana replied that I would be there immediately. How strange ... he had come over without waiting for my phone call. I ran to the bathroom to wash up in a hurry. Then I put on a dress and I rushed downstairs. "I hadn't heard from you and didn't want to wake you up, so I waited but it got late so I came to pick you up." "Good! Thank you." This morning I slept like a log. We went to a restaurant with outdoor tables that were in the shade of large trees. A very special place. I was not hungry but I decided to eat anyway just to avoid the third degree (have you already eaten? and with whom have you been if Marco is never at the bar? etc.) Even though I'd already had breakfast, I had an appetizer of mussels and baked fish. After lunch I wanted to take a walk. " Don't you wear my ring anymore?" He asked. I blushed, and I immediately explained that I had hidden it at home to avoid bring it to work, it was too precious. And when he arrived so suddenly, I forgot to wear it. I had the feeling that something had cooled off between us. I decided to ignore it, though; instead, I acted nicer than usual. So I gave him a kiss and then I grabbed his hand to have a walk. He seemed satisfied and pleased. So when the shops opened we were in the front row. Immediately, I reminded him to buy condoms even though I didn't feel like making love to him at all. He enjoyed this gesture so much that he wanted to buy me gifts: so he asked me whether there was anything I needed. I bought a pair of comfortable black shoes with a medium heel, at another store I chose two dresses and finally I stopped in front of a lingerie shop. Here I said I wanted to surprise him. We walked in, he spoke to the clerk and told her that I needed to pick something, when I finished he would come to pay, so I could choose what I wanted, while he was smoking a cigarette outside. Just to make him happy and to help him relax a bit and also because that store had relly nice things, I got two very sexy intimate outfits and four pairs of stockings. Then I went out to call him to pay the bill. The shop was not cheap at all and as soon as we were alone

Remo asked me: "What did you buy to spend so much?" And I said "A couple of things to do two stripteases for you, aren't you happy?" On hearing this he got very excited or perhaps he already was since I had entered the store so he immediately took me to the hotel. Here, I got ready and I did an exceptional striptease just for him, I was wearing black fishnet stockings, black heeled shoes and a bra with parade straps. With a great desire after he put on a condom he penetrated me for a long time until he came. Realizing that I had not come yet, after washing up in the bathroom, he came back more excited than before and wearing protection he penetrated me from behind. With one hand he pulled me towards him and with the other he touched me in the front. He touched me so well that I came twice. He came only once while I was coming for the second time. We both took a shower. This time separately. I asked him if he wanted to go to the movies. He agreed. We watched an action movie. Then we went to dinner, I ate very little. He ate normally, as usual. We came back to the hotel. He wanted another striptease with the other outfit. Always wearing protection he took me from behind, touching me more intensely than before so I came more than twice. When I came, he stopped for a moment without coming out of me, he touched my nipples and then went back to touching me in front while slamming me stronger than before. Eventually, he came. He took a shower and then crashed. Instead, I could not sleep, I thought about how Rico was different from him, to the fact that he didn't need a striptease to love me so much. Max too didn't seem to need anithing more to get excited with me. Eventually, I fell asleep at about three o'clock.

August 28, Tuesday

Tuesday at dawn, as usual, the alarm went off. I also got up and got ready. We had breakfast, then Remo insisted that I should take the car. I took him to the resort and than I immediately went to Marco's to sleep some more. I woke up at lunchtime as usual. After lunch and after Tiziana had cleaned the kitchen, we went out like we were often used to, just to have a good chat. We brought with us little Luca in his stroller. I told Tiziana my thoughts about the stripteases that appealed so much to Remo. She just thought it could be a nice thing to do every now and then, and after all he had never asked me to do them. I was still puzzled anyway. I wished Remo didn't have any resemblance with the men who I met in that place. *Wake up, hunny, They're all men anyway!* Rico, however, was different! I spent the rest of the afternoon reading a book and watching TV. Around dinner time, Marco told me that I had a dinner date with a man. I asked him if I knew him, he was vague about it, and he told me he was ok and after dinner he would take me back to the nightclub. The whole thing seemed kind of strange to me. When had this man contacted Max and Marco? Tiziana reassured me saying that if his father wasn't worried, I could relax. I went to the appointment and I almost fainted when I saw that Rico was my date! "Did you like the surprise? I spoke with Marco and we agreed that you can spend all night with me. You'll be back tomorrow morning. Are you happy? "I was in seventh heaven! What a nice surprise! I Just didn't expect. I explained that I had made a lot of resistance to go on a date with a stranger at night but Marco assured me that after dinner the customer would immediately take me back to the club without any intermediate stops. Rico had booked dinner in the restaurant of the most luxurious hotel in Bellaria. There, if I wanted to, we could spend the night together. Wow! What a luxurious place! "I wanted to prove to you that you mean a lot to me and to apologize for the fact that I have always kept you in a car or on the beach for me while you deserve only the best places in the world!" He was very sweet! Dinner was delicious and I ate a forkful of everything. After dinner Rico asked me what I wanted to do and I told him I wanted to go in the room with him right away. He had already picked up the keys. He took me to a beautiful suite. Who knows how much he spent! After opening the door he picked me up and gently put me on the bed. He started to kiss me and caress me in such a loving way. I felt so drawn to him that I wanted something more. As if read my thoughts he said there was no rush and that we had the whole night for us. But he couldn't resist for too long. Suddenly, he took off only my panties and we made love. Then he went to the toilet. After a while he took me to the bathroom where he had a filled a hot jacuzzi, we hopped in. With a delicious bubble bath, he began to caress my whole body. At first we were one in front of the other then, he said we were too far apart he had me sit in front of him with my back against his chest. He kissed me on the neck, shoulders, as he continued to caress me everywhere. I was so excited that I no longer resisted. I had him sitting on the edge and I climbed over him. By holding me he brought me back to bed. He was the man of my life, I thought, he liked me as I was, he liked my 'position in bed' ... he was incredibly sweet! We spent the whole night making love. We just couldn't break away from each other. And we couldn't fall sleep. Best night of my life! We also talked a lot. I talked about Max's fake Rolex and fake diamonds business that. Rico was once again amazed. "Why did you tell me?" He asked. "Aren't you afraid I might seize the nightclub?" "No! It's for your career enhancement!". "In addition to being the most beautiful woman I've ever met, you manage to surprise me every day. But how do you do it?" "That's just the way I am!" We finally fell asleep around dawn. So when the alarm clock rang at six, he involuntarily picked up and hung up the phone, almost half asleep. At nine, on opening his eyes he quickly realized that it was very late. How could he not have heard the alarm?! So we got ready in a real hurry.

August 29, Wednesday

We were both very sad that our date was already over. Apologizing to me, he called a taxi. He gave me fifty thousand liras to pay for it. And we promised that we would see each other soon. I went home by taxi. They were already all awake. Tiziana wanted me to tell her the evening. She too was very surprised of the treatment that Rico had reserved for me. After all, he had to also support a wife and children with his salary ... he must have spent a fortune for an evening like that with me! Tiziana thought he really felt something special for me, but he was always a married man who would have never given up his children. "But I've never asked anything of him" I thought to myself, but I wanted so much to have the courage to ask him about us. Even this day went by quickly. In the evening I went to the club with Marco. In the middle of the night he came back home, he really didn't feel well once again. On the one hand I felt sorry for him, on the other hand I didn't want to be alone with Max. After what I had seen. He might as well stay with the Russians! *You're really out of it! Do you start a relationship with every man you meet?* Tonight there is lots of work. Fortunately, Giorgio, the guy with the bar came to see me. So we had a chat. I told him that I really liked his bar, and that he was an exquisite guy I felt at ease with. Perhaps he misunderstood my words and pulled a small package from his pocket. It was a ring and he asked me to be his woman. He would even allow me to keep on working there at the club. He only wanted me to move to his house. I really didn't know how to turn him down without hurting his feelings too much. So I gave him a sop. I started kissing and touching him. He let himself go and after a while he came. I went to the bathroom and when I returned I told him that I could not take such an important decision just like that. Anyway, in September I would be back to my house in Rome and there I had my parents who wanted me to graduate ... *So, you didn't turn him down because you had a boyfriend a lover and between them you sell your body for money ... Well, in fact it would have been shocking and particularly indelicate!* He felt bad but wanted at all costs that I accepted the ring. He didn't want to lose me. I told him that I would accept another kind of gift for the moment. He than left. Hopefully, he didn't take it too bad ... he is such a sweet boy. I had another few short tables. And I spent the last few hours with many girls on the sofas. Since there were almost no customers and Max, as often happened, was alone; he shut the place down early. He had the bouncer take the girls home so we were alone once again. "I'll tidy up a little and then I'll take you home, okay?" He said loudly just to be heard by the girls and the bouncer. "Yes, thank you!" I replied, thinking to myself that I really didn't want to be alone with him, I just didn't want to. So after a while that they were gone, Max came on to me. I tried to avoid him saying that I had my cycle and I didn't feel like it. "But you always go with the policeman! Why? "And I:" But don't you have your wife? And aren't all those Russian girls enough for you?" "Are you jealous? I really didn't expect it from you. Come here, only once, come on!" And, maybe because I was used to it or maybe because of the strong attraction I had for him, I gave in. Before, I went into the bathroom to remove the pad. Then he "fucked" me where he usually does on our sofa, which fortunately was not the one where I had seen him with the Russian. Anyway, I didn't come, whereas he did. We got dressed and then he took me to Marco's. Who knows, maybe after that ugly vision that I had, I could no longer relax enough to come with him. *Wait for another couple of days, you'll see … everything will be back to normal …*

August 30, Thursday

Max, as usual, wanted to take me to breakfast at the bar … I thanked him, but I was ok, I didn't feel like eating anything. I just wanted to go home, I wasn't feeling well. "I'm sorry! Hope it's not for what you saw! "I only said no. Then I was silent the whole trip. When we got home, I coldly said bye and quickly got out of the car. At home I tried to sleep but I just couldn't. Both Remo and Max seemed so strange, way different from what I had imagined. They were both somehow disappointing. Rico's situation saddened me, married with children, a situation he had purposely kept from me just to go to bed with me. I was very confused and bitter. Of course I couldn't tell what had happened between me and Max to anyone, not even Tiziana. Keeping this thing to myself created great discomfort inside of me. *What did you expect? To find the man of your life in a situation like that and behaving in such a way with many other men? Are you're still dreaming? … I really feel sorry for you though!* After a delicious lunch made by Laura of

85

which I only tasted a small piece of cake, we all had a short rest and then we all went to the club together. Laura began to do the cleaning with Marco, instead I, Tiziana and children went to Remo's resort. While we were in the sun with little Luca in the stroller under the beach umbrella, Marco came over to call me. He told me that the owner of the club wanted to talk to me. As soon as I entered the club Marco and the owner gave me the third degree to know about Max: whether I had seen him flirting with the girls or if the girls had told me something or even if I had been to bed with him. I quietly denied everything. *By now you've become a perfect liar!* Then the owner changed the subject and he almost begged me to stay. He told me that he owned other nightclubs and that if I was sick of the place I could also change. He would also increase the pay: he was willing to give me L. 2,500,000 every 2 weeks instead of one and a half million. Seeing me quite reluctant, he asked me at least to think about it. I told him that I would, and that and I really thanked him for his offer. Since the first part of the conversation where he accused Max had particularly stressed me out, I decided to stay there at Remo's resort. He knew my taste and prepared dinner for me: two hamburgers with salad. I ate some and I gave the rest to Perlina. I waited to go to the nightclub and to start work right on time. When I arrived I felt somewhat nervous. Marco and the bouncer were both standing at the entrance, Max however, was talking to the owner. So that will serve him just right! What need was there to go with the Russians before opening time? *What a possessive girl, are you jealous of him too?* Maybe I'm still angry with him. I just hoped he would have a special relationship only with me, at least inside the club, but I was wrong. I had already done a few tables when I saw the guy of the pools coming back. He asked me almost immediately if he could take me to lunch the next day as the last time. I said: "It depends!" Then he asked me: "From what?" I replied: "If this time you'll use a condom, if now at least you'll buy a bottle and if instead of three hundred thousand liras you give me four hundred for tomorrow. It's the least you can do, to be forgiven! What do you say?" He accepted everything, but he wanted in exchange a sign of peace: he wanted me to touch him. I obviously accepted. He ordered a bottle of average price and then we moved to a more private sofa. I then started to touch him, but he pushed my head on his penis. I wriggled away and told him that if he wanted this further service he was to give me another hundred thousand right there and then. He must have been particularly horny because he immediately gave me the money out of his wallet. I began to lick him, he wanted to come into my mouth, but I shunned it just the right moment! *By now you've become a real pro!* I didn't like his way of doing things. What a stress! Fortunately he calmed down a bit, but right at the end of time the bottle he took my hand again. He wanted me to touch him again! Knowing that his bottle time had almost run out I pointed out that the waiters would come very soon for the new order and, therefore there was not enough time left for that. So, when Max came over, the guy ordered yet another drink. Then, just to get it over with, I immediately started to touch him: I really didn't want to compromise our date for the day after. As usual, he came immediately. I went to the bathroom to wash my hands. Then he said goodbye confirming our date for the next day. At about two o'clock Rico came to pick me up. We went to our usual spot, the pine forest by the sea. As the car stopped Rico too decided to give me the TENTH degree! He definitely kept me under pressure at for at least half an hour storming me with countless questions asking me the same things over and over again just to see if I would contradict myself. I fortunately I never did. *Yes, little Mata Hari!* I eventually asked if all those questions he was asking me were work related or just because he was jealous. He, who wasn't expecting to be forced to answer any questions at that time, was definitely caught off guard, and he leaked out that it was also a matter of work. Then, he suddenly started kissing me and touching me in a somewhat different way from the usual: he was much more impulsive and way less sweet than ever. Shortly after, he was inside me, and while we were making love, he asked me "What is it... you don't love me any more? You just want your customers now? Don't you want me like before?" Just after he said these words he came. I was really puzzled, I said: "What's the matter?" Pushing him away from my body as a small tear fell on my cheek. Seeing me sohe grabbed my hands and began to apologize to me, saying he was too jealous of my work ... I had to leave it as soon as possible and that knowing I was at the nightclub he could no longer concentrate on his work. He was afraid that someone else would touch me, kiss me or that something like that would happen. So we started talking. He claimed to have lost his head for me and loved me and he didn't think he could do without me. But I reminded him he had to think of his children, his family. Rico became silent and began to give me his usual tender kisses and cover me with caresses. After a while I wanted to make love, but didn't want to take the initiative. He, on the other hand seemed to expect me to say something. I couldn't think of anything, so I said "What's the matter, don't you want me anymore?" But with a sickly sweet tone. So Rico quietly now resumed to make love to me, this time as usual, as we both liked. Just like sweethearts do. And, without any words, we tried to use every moment to love eachother, giving mutual pleasure to each other for countless times until the break of dawn. It was already time to leave and, while we were getting dressed I took a picture of him. "You always manage to surprise me ... I did'nt expect it!" He said. "I wanted to keep a little memory of you!" I put my hand over the shift stick, under his hand while he was driving. So, that way we arrived at Marco's home. "Try to get some rest!" He said. "You too, if you can, bye."

August 31, Friday

Shortly after coming back home, as the new family had things to do that morning, I decided to take my mind off all the new thoughts that assailed me for a while and go see George, the guy of the bar by myself, all alone. *Of course, getting involved with a fourth man was exactly what you needed!* I was confused, I knew that I would shorty be leaving to come back to Rome. I wondered if I would see Rico ever again. Would he do anything to be with me? Would he somehow manage to find the excuse, the time, the way to see me again? I arrived at Giorgio's bar with these thoughts on my mind. He was really delighted to see me, fortunately, there were so many people in the bar so it wasn't possible for him to propose to me once again. Just like the last time he said I could have anything I wanted. Not having had any breakfast I had cappuccino and a simple croissant. I invited him to come see me that night at the club. He was hesitant ... who knows if he will? If you don't see each other again before I leave, too bad for him. Then, knowing that I was about to go back to Rome and with the idea to thank my new family for their hospitality, I took a short trip to a nearby mall where I bought a food processor. It had a whole lot of functions and so many pieces. I hope they like it! I then went back home. My new little family hadn't come back yet. I put the well wrapped box with the gift inside on the kitchen table. Since nobody was showing up, I took a bath. I was just out of the bathroom and I was drying my hair when everyone came back. When they went in the kitchen with their shopping bags, they immediately saw the gift box. I peaked in and said that I hoped that this small gift would be helpful. I chose a food processor because I had heard Laura complain about having to cut a lot of vegetables in hand, having to knead the mixture of cakes or pizza. They were all very pleasantly surprised. Marco said that, once again, he wouldn't ask for any percentage for the second fortnight of work at the club because I was too kind and generous. Just as well! Knowing that most likely this afternoon would be one of the last I spent with them, at least for this summer I tried to impress all of them in my memory to never forget them again. I was confident that I would be back to visit them or they would come and see me in Rome, but in life you never know. Damn, I'd forgotten the appointment with the guy of the pools. Hopefully he won't show up at the club to complain. As usual Tiziana helped me prepare for the evening with tender loving care. Even Laura combed my hair just like a loving mother does to her daughter. They all had dinner, but I didn't touch any food because my stomach was closed. Max was already at the club, so was the bouncer and many girls. Max was as always dressed in a gaudy suit. He was charming and smelled very good as usual. I also noticed that he was very nervous. I wonder if his nervousness was due to the fact that he had to defend himself against Marco's accusations of forcing all the girls in the nightclub to sleep with him against their will. All in all, if the owner kept him there it meant he trusted him, or just that he was a person you could always count on, as opposed to Marco who was away quite often and was rather unreliable. I did a little of tables with fairly normal customers. Then the secret agent showed up. I couldn't believe how could this man could have the nerve to show his face at this club and ask of me so shamelessly. I was very angry with him. I had been cheated and taken for a ride. Anyway, I was still going to do my job. We sat on a somewhat private sofa. He saw that I was very angry he tried to give me explanations. He claimed that his daughter thinking he went with prostitutes was one of his many strategies to not reveal his real job in intelligence. Anyhow, I would never be able to believe his words again. *Wait for a couple of days when you cool off and then you'll see ...* We ordered a drink and, since I was rather nervous, I ordered an alcoholic one. Max, knowing my drinking habits, was rather surprised. With his sweet talk he was trying to confuse me and make me answer new questions. However I was still working and I thought I would soon be back in Rome, I managed to answer being quite vague about what I was saying. So, I guess I missed the fact that during the entire period I had spent in the nightclub I had discovered something of illegal. He tried to get me to say more things. After some time, as if he was trying to give me some kind of explanation, he said something like, "That's why they are preparing a task force to trap a gang of fences of counterfeit valuable goods!" Realizing that these last words had surprised me, he went more in detail. He said it was likely that this sort of raid would take place that very night. In addition they would also raid and search the whole place, including the girls. Seeing that I showed some concern about what he had just informed me about, he adviced me to try to leave the place as soon as possible. He gave me an appointment at the public beach near Remo's resort. He would be waiting for me at one o'clock. If I went, I could release my statement of all the facts of which I was aware of. Such statement would be a good start for my future career as a secret agent. I just couldn't trust his words anymore. But what he said was very strange. He seemed to be referring to Max's activity I had earlier revealed to Rico. Was Rico behind a possible incursion? If that were the case, however, I think he would have informed me and would not have allowed me to go to the nightclub that night. Besides, the strange agent had started by kind of courting me, saying that he had been very well with me, that I was beautiful and that I was very good in bed even though he hadn't even come! Well! While he was saying all these things to me he was also trying to make some sort contact with me ... *or maybe with every girl!?* ... Starting from touching my hands. But I remained professional, detached so after about four drinks he left and said, "Remember, I'll be waiting for you on the beach!" Though I could not completely believe those things he had told me, I was a bit worried. I didn't want to get in any trouble. *But do you really believe all this? Weren't 30 days enough to understand the kind of crowd that hangs around the club?* My anxiety increased, also because I saw Max increasingly nervous as if was expecting something bad to happen. Luckily, I was on the sofas in front of the dance floor along with some girls when Giorgio, the bar guy, joined me. I was quite happy to see him ... surely he would be able to help me out. It was about 11:55. If I were to believe that agent, I would have to do something soon enough. I took Giorgio in a private sofa. Max, as usual, came to take the order. After bringing us our drinks Giorgio and I started talking. Or rather, I wanted to talk to him and instead we made out for some time with the excuse that maybe I would soon be leaving, and who knows when we might have the chance to see each other again and that he had great desire for me. He got really horny and he wouldn't listen to me unless I pampered him a little. So we kissed as he tried to put his hands all over me. His mouth was soft as usual, but I just couldn't relax, I was too worried. I immediately took the initiative and when I unbuttoned his pants, I started to touch him. He also touched me with his hand tucked under my skirt. Fortunately, thanks to my little experience I had gained during this month I was quite skillfull. So George came almost immediately. At this point, I insisted that he should pay attention to what I was saying, telling him that I would explain everything at the bar the next day. I asked him to do me a huge favor. Max came out of nowhere and asked us if we have another drink something else: it was our second drink. Fortunately

Giorgio had just buttoned up his pants. As soon as the drinks were served, I started talking with Giorgio and asked him if, as soon he had finished his drink, he could go to a specific beach resort where he would have to contact Remo, a friend of mine, and tell him that I was waiting for him at the nightclub for a very important matter. *Now you need Remo... you go to him to put things right, because you know that you can trust him, so now he is useful!* Although he couldn't quite understand what was going on, he was pushed by what I had done and by my promise to explain everything the day afer at his bar; he agreed to help me out. When Max came over he said he had to leave. In my heart I was hoping I wouldn't do any table until Remo would arrive. To use up some more time I went to the bathroom and I stayed there for a while. Certainly much more than usual. Fortunately, when I went back on the floor, Remo had arrived. We did the table to talk. I was almost in tears when I told him that I needed help, that I was risking a lot and he had to pay for me to leave. So Remo paid for my departure and so we went to talk on a bench in front of the beach. I tried to explain almost everything. In tears, *(Crocodile tears, too easy to cry now)* I confessed that I had been with Max once and that on that occasion I was then taken to a parking lot where he sold fake diamonds and Rolexes. I had then foolishly told a police officer who hung around the nightclub about it and that a guy who had me thinking he was working for the secret services had taken advantage of me. And that night he had come to the nightclub and told me to go on the beach to give out a statement where I would tell everything I knew about that and finally that the nightclub would surely be raided by Police for a thorough search and investigation. As he felt I had betrayed him too, Remo started crying just like me. Then he asked me what time that guy had given me appointment at. I told him between midnight and one. My confession actually lasted a really long time. Remo pointed out that this man, the secret agent had had me once again. It was 2:30 in the morning by then. *Good morning, well awakened from the world of fairy tales, come back to earth, come down from the clouds!* I told him that I was really sorry and that I wanted to seriously be only with him and that I loved him. He told me he loved me too. "Let's start all over again, okay?" He said. I gladly accepted. "Soon I'll take you to the club to get your paycheck for your last two weeks of work, then I'll take you home. When you've rested a bit, start packing. I'll lend you my car go straight home to Rome and wait for me there. I'll be back on September 15. We're leaving for Paris together, and we can start all over again What do you say? "" It would be a dream! I love you! I can't wait to be with you in Paris, I love that city it's beautiful! But are you're sure You love me? Even after what I told you? "" Yes! I'm not the kind of man who loves any woman he goes to bed with! "" I really love you, you're so naive, helpless! *"Obviously being lucky is one of the characteristics that follows you in life!*

September 1, Saturday

I did as Remo had suggested. We went together to the nightclub to get the pay for the two weeks. They gave me three million two hundred fifty thousand. Remo spoke in my place saying that I had a problem at home and unfortunately I had to go back to Rome immediately. So they didn't try to convince me to stay. I asked Remo if he could take me to the bank to send the money to my mother. So we went there too. Then, he drove me to Marco's home. There, I really couldn't fall asleep so I had a chat with Tiziana. I told her that Remo had found out about my work and that I had cutomers outside of the nightclub. I did not want lose him so I left my job that very night. First, I would go to Rome. And then, Remo would take me to Paris to start all over again from scratch and build our new, healthy relationship. I was happy about that, but sad to leave all of them especially her, Tiziana. I packed up and, after saying goobye in tears to my whole new family, I drove over to Remo's. He just wanted to feel that I would be ok so he filled up his car's tank, gave me the registration card and then he insisted I take 600,000 liras with me. I might need them. I agreed, although I knew I had quite a stash of money from my extra work with me, but I just couldn't tell him that. Absolutely not! So after a long kiss and after writing down directions all the way to Rome for me, we said goodbye. "Call me when you arrive! I love you! "He said. "I love you a lot too!" I replied. Then I finally left. On the highway, however, I sometimes realized I was still thinking about Rico. Would I be able to really forget him? And would he actually forget me? I didn't know what kind future was waiting for me although it apparently seemed to have already been written. I had a very long journey. I finally arrived home. My folks wanted to talk with me about my stay in Bellaria but I was too tired and confused to do just that and so I went staight to my room with the excuse that I was exhausted by the long drive. However, instead of falling asleep I started fantasizing and remembering Rico and what we had lived together ... and then Remo ... I really felt very confused. I'm tired of writing. So I'll stop for a while. So long, diary! Tomorrow I'll find a good place to hide you. I really wouldn't want anybody to find you.

Goodnight Rico, I'll miss you so much!

You really are quite a strange creature. A bit confused?! You end your diary thinking about Rico! Of course it's impossible for us to understand you ... We who are "mere mortals"! The actual victim, with all our compassion is Remo! We would have liked an ending dedicated to him ... But after all, this is just your first diary ... I wonder how many more surprises you've got for us! And then ... Who's to say that wonderful things won't happen to Remo in the future? And who knows, maybe Mizzy will actually get her act together some day!

INDEX

Finito di stampare nel mese di Novembre 2015
per conto di Youcanprint *self - publishing*

www.ingramcontent.com/pod-product-compliance
Lightning Source LLC
Chambersburg PA
CBHW080748250626
47162CB00010B/3065